Caitlin Crews

Greek's Last Redemption

D0357640

⊕ HARLEQUIN PRESENTS®

ISBN-13: 978-0-373-13335-2

Greek's Last Redemption

First North American Publication 2015

Copyright © 2015 by Harlequin Books S.A.

Special thanks and acknowledgment are given to Caitlin Crews for her contribution to The Chatsfield series.

Recycling programs for this product may not exist in your area.

Printed in U.S.A.

www.Harlequin.com

USA TODAY bestselling author and RITA® Award-nominated author **Caitlin Crews** loves writing romance. She teaches her favorite romance novels in creative writing classes at places like UCLA Extension's prestigious Writers' Program, where she finally gets to utilize the MA and PhD in English literature she received from the University of York in England. She currently lives in California with her very own hero and too many pets. Visit her at caitlincrews.com.

Books by Caitlin Crews
Harlequin Presents

At the Count's Bidding
Undone by the Sultan's Touch
Not Just the Boss's Plaything
A Devil in Disguise
In Defiance of Duty
The Replacement Wife
Princess from the Past

Vows of Convenience
His for Revenge
His for a Price

Royal & Ruthless
A Royal without Rules

Scandal in the Spotlight
No More Sweet Surrender
Heiress Behind the Headlines

Self-Made Millionaires
Katrakis's Last Mistress

Bride on Approval
Pure Princess, Bartered Bride

Visit the Author Profile page
at Harlequin.com for more titles.

To Pippa Roscoe,
for being her fabulous self, especially in Texas.

And to Kelly Conroy,
for sharing her Barcelona with me.
I hope I brought it to life, at least a little bit!

CHAPTER ONE

THEO TSOUKATOS SCOWLED when his office door swung open despite the fact he'd given strict orders that he wasn't to be disturbed. He expected his orders to be followed—and they usually were, because no one who worked for him enjoyed the consequences when they were not.

He was becoming more like his widely feared father by the day, he thought grimly. Which he could tolerate as long as that was only true here, in the business sphere. God help him if he ever acted like his father in his personal life.

Never, he vowed, as he had since he was a child. *I will never let that happen.*

"I trust the building is on fire?" he asked his secretary icily as she marched inside, because it could only be a crisis that brought her in here against his instructions, surely. He glowered at her. "Or is about to be?"

"Not as far as I'm aware," she retorted, appearing utterly unperturbed by his aggressive tone. Mrs. Papadopoulos, who reminded him of his hatchet-faced, steely-haired and pursed-mouthed aunt and acted about as enamored of Theo as Aunt Despina always had been, was meant to keep him from distractions rather than cause them. "But it's early yet."

Theo sighed his impatience. He was in the middle of compiling the rest of his notes on fuel efficiency and trim optimization strategies for the meeting that he'd be running in his father's stead today, now that wily old Demetrious Tsoukatos was focusing more on his mounting medical issues than on the family business. He glanced out the wall of windows surrounding him and saw all of Athens arrayed at his feet, the sprawling commotion and hectic madness of the greatest city in Greece serving as a reminder, the way it always did.

That all that rose must fall—before rising again, stronger than before.

That was the unspoken Tsoukatos family creed. It was the story of Theo's own life, certainly. It was built into every inch of the proud Tsoukatos tower, where Theo now sat. Just like the steel girders themselves that made the building an imposing physical testament to his shipping magnate father's searing vision and ruthless success in the face of all obstacles, from sworn enemies to the faltering economy.

These days, the tower stood as a marker of Theo's own growing reputation as a fearless risk taker and out-of-the-box thinker in a business cluttered by those who played it safe straight into bankruptcy. That wasn't going to happen to the Tsoukatos fleet. Theo might have acted the spoiled heir apparent for most of his twenties, but in the past four years he'd dedicated himself to proving he was every bit as formidable and intimidating as the old man himself.

It turned out he was good at this. As if ruthless power really did run in his veins the way his father had always assured him it did. Or should.

And he'd decided he could emulate his father here, in the boardroom, where that kind of ruthlessness was a positive thing. Theo's own personal life might have been a mess, such as it was, but not for the same reasons Demetrious's had been. *I may not be happy*, he often told himself fiercely, *but at least I'm not a liar, a cheater or a hypocrite*.

He was surrounded by too many who couldn't say the same.

Theo aimed his most ferocious glare at Mrs. Papadopoulos as she came to a sharp stop on the other side of his wide desk. She eyed him right back with her special brand of mild judgment and automatic condemnation, which, perversely, he quite enjoyed. The woman was his own, personal version of the proverbial hair shirt and Theo was nothing if not the kind of man who liked to keep his sins as close as possible to his skin.

"It's your wife," Mrs. Papadopoulos said crisply, speaking of his sins, and Theo stopped enjoying himself. With a great thud that he was momentarily worried was actually audible.

His wife.

Holly.

Theo was so used to that flare of dark rage, that thunderbolt of pure fury, that he told himself he hardly noticed it any longer as it careened through him, setting off a string of secondary explosions. It had been almost four whole years since he'd laid eyes on his errant wife. Almost four years since they'd been in the same room, or even in the same country. Four years since he'd last touched her, tasted her, lost himself in her—which he never would again, he reminded himself coldly, as it was, not coincidentally, also four years since he'd discovered the truth about her. And the mockery she'd made of their marriage.

You did not discover *the truth about her*, he reminded himself darkly. Pointedly. *She presented her confession to you, as if on a silver platter...*

But God help him, he couldn't let himself go down that dark path. Not today. Not here, in his place of business, where he had become renowned for his icy calm under any and all forms of pressure. Not anymore.

Not ever again.

He should have been over this by now, Theo thought then, the way he always did. But instead he had to order himself to breathe, to unclench his fists, to relax the instant, furious tautness of his body against his chair and pretend he was as unmoved as he should have been after all this time.

"If it is *my wife*, then I am not only busy, I am uninterested," he said, making no attempt to hide the crack of temper in his voice. "You know better than to bother me with such drivel, Mrs. Papadopoulos. *My wife* is to be diverted to voice mail or email, which I check as little as possible and certainly no more than once every—"

"Sir." And Theo didn't know what surprised him more. That the woman dared interrupt him or that, when he stared at her in astonishment, the rigid yet normally obedient Mrs. Papadopoulos stood her ground. "She insists that it's an emergency."

The last thing in the world Theo wanted to think about, today or ever, was Holly. His downfall—the more uncharitable might call her his comeuppance, and in his darker moments he found he agreed, because he'd married a liar just like the one he'd sworn he'd never become—in one smooth and deceitful and much too pretty female form.

Because the sad truth was that he already spent a significant portion of every day *not* thinking about her. His predawn hours in his private gym, beating his endless fury into the hanging bag or the occasional sparring partner. The brutal miles he logged on his treadmill. *Not* thinking about her betrayal of him with, she'd told him so distinctly, some tourist whose name she hadn't bothered to catch. *Not* imagining those same sickening scenes over and over again, all etched into his brain as if he'd actually witnessed her betrayal himself. *Not* wondering how he could have fallen so completely for the lies she'd told him when he should have known better, when he should have been far too jaded to be taken in by her artless little act…

For four years he'd thrown himself into the family business with the express purpose of thinking of something other than the lying, cheating creature he'd married so foolishly and the many ways she'd ruined him. She'd made him a laughingstock. That smarted, but she'd also ripped out the heart he'd never been aware he'd possessed before her. *That* was infinitely worse. And more than that, she'd tricked him into re-enacting his own parents' doomed marriage, which he couldn't find it in him to forgive. For four years he'd focused all of the *feelings* he refused to call by name into something tangible: the comprehensive decimation of all Tsoukatos business rivals and the unquestionable success of the company against what should have been insurmountable odds in these troubled times.

No one had called Theo Tsoukatos, once a proud member of Europe's entitled dilettante contingent with the notches on his bedpost to prove it, a spoiled and pampered playboy in a very long while. No one would dare.

But Holly was his living, breathing, walking and talking failure. The crowning achievement of his wasted youth. The embodiment of the pointless creature he'd been back then, a grave disappointment to his father and an epic, permanent stain upon his family name.

He did not want to think about how hard he'd fallen for the dizzy little blonde thing from the United States who'd pretended to adore him at first sight, how desperately he'd pursued her after their initial week together on the island or how deeply and callously she'd betrayed him a mere six months after the wedding that he'd been blind enough to consider romantic not despite its speed but because of it.

He especially did not want to recollect the unpleasant truth: that he had no one to blame for any of these things but himself.

Everyone had warned him, after all. At length. Everyone save Theo had seen supposedly gauche and charmingly naive Holly Holt, touring Europe all on her own following her father's death, for exactly who and what she was. One more American gold digger with Texas dirt on her feet and her calculating blue eyes set on the biggest and best catch she could find.

On Santorini that summer, that catch had been Theo.

"You are my successor and the heir to the Tsoukatos fortune," his father had told him sternly, over and over again and to no avail. "This girl is nobody. This can never be anything more than a holiday romance, Theo. You must understand this."

His father and his brother, Brax, had lined up to tell him not to be a fool, but Theo had hardly been inclined to take advice from the man who'd destroyed Theo's own mother with his infidelities, much less a younger brother he'd thought of then as little more than a child. And then, when it was clear that he was determined to prove himself a colossal fool, anyway, they'd begged him to *at the very least* take the necessary steps to protect his fortune, his future, the company, on the off chance that he was thinking with his groin instead of his head… And Theo had ignored them all, the way he always had done throughout his hedonistic twenties, because he'd cared about nothing and no one but himself.

Nothing but himself and one curvy little blonde girl with deep blue eyes to rival the Aegean Sea itself. She'd had the widest, sweetest, most open smile he'd ever seen, and he'd lost himself in it. In her. And there had been nothing, it turned out, but a deceitful heart beneath all that sweet shine.

This, then, was his reward for his impetuousness. His penance. This humiliation of a marriage that he held on to only because he refused to give her the satisfaction of asking for a divorce, despite what she'd done to him and then thrown in his face so unapologetically. He refused to let her see how she'd destroyed him over the course of that long, rainy season on Santorini years ago.

It had been nearly four and a half years since they'd married in far too much haste in the height of the dry Greek summer, almost four whole years since they'd been within the same walls, and Theo thought he was still coldly furious enough to stretch it out to ten, if necessary. He might not want her any longer, he might have vowed to himself that he would fling himself from the Santorini cliffs before he'd let her work her evil magic on him again, but he'd be damned if he'd let her have her freedom from him unless she begged for it.

Preferably at length and on her knees. He was a simple man. An eye for an eye, and a humiliation for a humiliation.

"*My wife* has never had a minor upset she couldn't

fluff up into a full-scale catastrophe," Theo bit out now, venting his spleen on his rigid secretary and not much minding if it made her bristle visibly. He paid her a not-inconsiderable fortune to tolerate him and his many black moods, after all. It was a great pity he hadn't taken the same amount of precautions when choosing his first wife. "Her version of an emergency generally involves her credit limit."

"I think this is different, Mr. Tsoukatos."

Theo was losing what little patience he had left—a virtue for which he was not widely renowned to begin with. This was already far more focused and specific attention paid to Holly and thus his marriage than he liked to permit himself outside the stark truths he otherwise faced only in his gym. He could see emails piling up in his inbox out of the corner of his eye, he still had to sketch out the rest of his presentation and the last thing in the world he had time for was his own, personal albatross and whatever her latest scheme was.

"Why?" he asked, aware that his voice was unduly hostile when Mrs. Papadopoulos stiffened further, a feat which should have been anatomically impossible. He shrugged. "Because she said so? She always does."

"Because she's videoed in." Mrs. Papadopoulos placed the tablet Theo hadn't noticed she was carrying down in the center of his desk. "Here you are." She stepped back, and her voice was as crisp as the look in her eyes was steely. "Sir."

Theo blinked, then eyed the tablet—and the frozen image there—as if Holly herself might leap forth

from the screen and stick another knife deep into his
back. Deeper this time, no doubt. Perhaps a killing
blow at last. It took him a moment to remember that
Mrs. Papadopoulos still stood there, exuding her typical brusque disapproval, and when he did he waved
her off before he betrayed himself any further.

A video call was certainly different. That was the
truth.

And when it came to Holly, "different" was never
good. "Different" always came with a heavy price
and Theo always ended up paying it.

She was his costliest mistake, by far. Of all the
many follies of his overindulged and deeply entitled
youth, Holly Holt from somewhere as improbable to
him as Texas ranch country, with the wide smile and
the big laugh that had broken him wide-open and left
him nothing but a goddamned fool in a thousand dis-
carded pieces, was the one he regretted most.

And daily, whether he permitted himself to think
about her directly or not.

"Control yourself," he snapped out loud, glaring
down at the tablet on the polished expanse of his
desk before him.

He moved to end the call without taking it, the way
he knew he should, but her image taunted him. Even
frozen into place and slightly pixelated, she was like
a hammer to the side of his head. He could feel her
everywhere, her claws still in him, deep.

Hating himself for his weakness didn't do a
damned thing to change it.

And she wasn't the raw, unformed creature she'd

been when he'd met her, all sun-kissed limbs and that unsophisticated beauty that he'd found so intoxicating. So mesmerizing. He studied the frozen image before him as if it might offer him a clue to her—to the truth of her he'd spent years telling himself she'd already shown him. Gone was the exuberant hair, the cowboy boots she'd once told him she loved more than most people, the open and carefree expression that had made her shine brighter than the Santorini sun.

She'd grown sleeker over the past few years. He'd seen it in the photographs he couldn't always avoid, scattered in this or that paper, but it was more obvious now that he was looking at her directly. That curvy figure of hers that had once made a simple bikini into a lush little scandal and had made him her slave bordered on skinny now. Her hair was still that sunny blond but it was straight and ruthlessly slicked back into a tasteful chignon today, her cosmetics minimal and wholly lacking in the sparkle or too-bright colors he remembered. Her dress was a masterful little exploration of classic, understated elegance and suited this new version of her perfectly.

Holly Holt was gone. Theo doubted she'd ever truly existed.

In her place was this woman. This shrewdly manufactured, ruthlessly accessorized creature. Holly Tsoukatos, who was such a committed philanthropist indeed with her absent husband's money forever at her disposal, he thought derisively. Holly Tsoukatos, who'd made herself known as the gracefully estranged wife of one of Europe's favorite former playboys, and who'd become more and more fashionable and sought after now that Theo was regarded as a force as dangerous and successful as his famous father.

He hated her, he told himself then, and he hated this. And most of all he hated the fact that he still wanted that gloriously over-the-top, unrestrained and uncultured little American girl who'd captivated a seasoned sophisticate like him in a single searing week.

But, of course, that Holly had been a lie. Why couldn't he remember that? She had never existed outside the virtuoso performance she'd put on for him four and a half years ago. *This* version of his wayward wife, this studiously well-mannered ice queen who'd built herself an entire little empire of lies thanks to his money and her commitment to spending it, was the real Holly. Staring at her frozen image, Theo acknowledged the fact that he didn't like remembering that harsh truth—it was one of the reasons he'd only spoken to her on the telephone and very rarely at that these past four years.

That and his unwieldy temper, which she alone seemed able to kick-start and send into overdrive with very little effort. But he hauled that dark, simmering, betrayed thing in him under control again, and he didn't care if it left marks as he did it. He'd rather die than show her anything but his dislike—the colder and more distant, the better. It wasn't the only thing she'd earned from him, not by a long shot, but it was the only thing he'd allow her to see.

He hit the button to unfreeze her and didn't bother masking his irritation.

"What do you want?" he said by way of greeting after all these years of nothing but infrequent telephone calls. His voice was blunt and unfriendly and even that wasn't enough to assuage the lick of his fury, that deep and dark current of a primal need to strike back at her however he could. "Have you managed to bankrupt me yet?"

This video call was a serious tactical error.

Holly realized it the moment the screen before her burst into life and color and sound again. Her courage and her determination—and much worse, her voice—deserted her in a sudden rush. *This was a terrible mistake*, the latest in a long line of terrible mistakes where this man was concerned...

Because she wasn't prepared for *him* in all his almost violent perfection. She never had been.

Because he was *Theo* and he was *right there* on her enormous desktop computer monitor after all these years, big and brooding and *beautiful*, bursting straight into her lonely little life with all that force and fire...

And he was still so very angry with her.

So deeply, encompassingly, seethingly angry, it felt like being plunged into a dark cloud without his having to say a single word. Though the words hurt, too—harsh and furious, each like a separate slap.

Looking at him was like a contact sport. It always

had been. It was worse now, with all that fury making him seem to *burn* right there before her eyes.

Holly had heard it on the phone during their short and hostile calls regarding her deliberately outrageous credit card bills these past years—always spaced out according to his ever more busy schedule, one per quarter at most and never long enough for any kind of real discussion. But now she could *see* it, burning like a fierce heat in his eyes as dark as the Greek coffee he'd made for her back in the early days of their brief marriage, before she'd ruined everything.

She could see it stamped in the fascinating iron set of his harshly masculine jaw, could even feel it deep inside her own body, like a shiver. Like a seismic warning. As if she should count herself lucky indeed that they were separated by computer screens, the internet and some six thousand miles.

As if he wouldn't be responsible for what happened if they were ever in the same room again, and Holly felt suspended in the thick, dark promises she could see in the furious heat he trained on her then, the glare of all that threat and power and fury, even after all this time.

What did you expect? that little voice inside of her that sounded a lot like her beloved father's, God rest his soul, whispered then. *He hates you. You made sure of that. That's what happens when you leave.*

She should know that better than most, after living through all those long, lonely years with her father after her mother's defection when Holly had been a little girl. Her father wouldn't have called how he'd mourned his wife's betrayal *hatred*, of course. He'd have called it grief. Or holding a torch. But Holly had always felt it like a burning thing, changing their whole world. Charring what was left.

And now here she was, all these years later, staring at that same fire directed straight at her. In high-definition.

Theo lounged before her in a leather chair in a sleekly furnished office, his thick, dark hair looking disheveled and too long, the way it always had. He was more beautiful than she remembered him, and she remembered him as very nearly a god with all that lean, leashed power packed into his solid boxer's form, as if he could have been a fighter had he been the son of a man with lower aspirations. He wore a crisp white shirt that strained to contain his corded, solid shoulders, that wonder of a chest and the tautly ridged abdomen she knew lay beneath. He looked powerful and furious and his own, special brand of lethal, and Holly hated herself all over again.

For what she'd done. For what she'd *claimed* she'd done. For the great big mess that was her whirlwind, ill-conceived, overwhelming marriage to this man and that big old dark hole in the center of everything that she'd come to realize was pure and nauseating *regret*. Greasy and enveloping, and so thick she truly believed it might choke her one of these days.

Though it never did. Not quite.

Instead, worse, she had to live with it.

She wanted to reach forward, through the screen, and test the heat of his smooth olive skin against her palms again. She wanted to run her fingers through his thick, dark hair and play with that hint of curl that had always made her silly with desire. She wanted to taste that full and talented mouth of his again, salt and fire, longing and need.

But there was no easy road here. Holly knew that. There was no way back to Theo that wouldn't rip open old scars and make ancient wounds bleed fresh. That wouldn't hurt, and badly. She'd been so terrified of becoming like her father that she'd become her mother instead, and she couldn't live with that any longer. *She couldn't.* She had to try to do something about it, no matter what.

Holly had thought she'd accepted how hard this was going to be already—but that had been before she'd *seen* him again. Somehow, the years had dulled him in her memory. Dimmed him.

Seeing him again, even through a screen, was as blinding as the first time she'd laid eyes on him. In that tiny restaurant in Santorini where she'd been sipping an afternoon coffee, unaware that her entire life had been set to collide with his when he'd shouldered his way inside and claimed the table next to hers.

Like a comet, she'd thought then, even on a sun-drenched Greek island with nothing but dizzying blue and whitewashed walls on all sides and then this man in the middle of it all, like a dream come to startling and powerfully sexy life…

"Holly."

His voice tore into her, dark and impatient and yet still, that little lilt to her name that made her whole

body shimmer into instant, almost painful awareness.
She was glad he couldn't see the way she tensed in
her seat in automatic reaction, her legs going tight as
she dug her toes into the floor beneath her desk. Or
that bright little light inside she knew was the most
dangerous, most doomed, thing of all. *Hope.*

"I don't have time for this today. And even if I did,
I have nothing to say to you." His hard mouth moved
into some lethal approximation of a smile, and her
curse was, it made him no less attractive to her. Quite
the opposite. "Nothing polite, that is."

It was so tempting to simply lose herself in him, or
to let herself break down and start telling the truths
she already knew he wouldn't believe, not when she'd
spent these long years trying so hard to force him to
let her go by any means possible. She'd made him
detest her, if not release her. She had to remember
the game she needed to play here or she'd lose before she started.

So Holly smiled at him. Not the way she once
had, when she hadn't had the faintest shred of self-
preservation in her body, when she hadn't been able
to *help* herself from falling into him and for him
like the proverbial ton of bricks, her innocence indis-
tinguishable from her stupidity, to her recollection.
But the way she'd perfected in these past few lonely
years, the smile that made it possible to play the role
she'd created for herself out of the ashes of the marriage she'd burned to the ground with her lies. The
role she'd thought would make it so simple for him

to wash his hands of her, to discard her, to divorce her and free them both.

She'd been wrong about that, too. She'd finally, painfully, faced the fact that she'd been wrong about everything, and that she'd done nothing here but re-enact her own painful history. But he wouldn't believe her if she told him that. He would think it was nothing more than another game, and he'd made it clear he wouldn't play them with her, hadn't he? Perfectly, coldly clear.

Which meant she had no choice but to play one last game with him, this one with the highest stakes of all.

"Busy?" she asked, letting her drawl take on a life of its own, a Texan specialty. "Doing what, exactly? Still playing the crown prince in your daddy's great big kingdom?"

Theo's expression went from furious to something like thunderstruck, then back to a hardness that should have left her in tatters. Maybe it did. Maybe the truth was that she couldn't tell the difference any longer.

"I beg your pardon?" His voice was icy, but there was no mistaking the threat beneath it. "I didn't realize it was time for our long-overdue conversation regarding each other's character flaws. Are you certain you're ready for that?"

"Blah blah blah," she said, rolling her eyes and waving a hand dismissively, wishing she felt even a tiny bit that relaxed or casual. "Just call me a whore already, Theo. You've been dancing around it for almost four years now."

CHAPTER TWO

THEO'S DARK EYES blazed to a molten fury and it amazed Holly that he could still make her lose her breath, that easily. Even when he thought so little of her.

And she was such a fool—because a sane woman, Holly knew, having done what she'd done, having lied so extravagantly in order to escape this man the only way she'd thought she could, would not have looked at that flare of fury in his dark eyes and read it as some sliver of hope for the future she'd torpedoed herself.

Because *fury* wasn't the same thing as indifference. Fury meant he still felt something for her, no matter how twisted and painful.

But then, Holly was aware that a sane woman wouldn't have gone ahead and married the dark Greek lover who'd swept her up in a kind of sensual tornado that summer, either, stealing her innocence and her heart and her good sense along with it. So maybe *sane* wasn't in the ballpark here.

Maybe she should stop pretending it had ever been a possibility where proximity to Theo was concerned.

"Let me guess," he said, his voice controlled in a way that made her wonder exactly how he'd grown in all these years. Exactly how he'd changed, when the Theo she'd known had been as impetuous and wild as he'd been rich and pampered. She'd been completely out of her league with this man from the start. "You decided to purchase a jet. An island. A couture house and half of Paris to go with it. I don't care, Holly. Your allowance is yours. Do what you want with it and leave me the hell alone."

He moved in his chair, his hand reaching toward her, and she knew he was about to end the call. That there was nothing tender there in that gesture, despite what it looked like for a brief second—what she wanted it to look like, fool that she still was.

"I want to see you," she said, before he could cut her off. Before she lost herself in these tiny little moments and the daydreams that went with them and completely forgot why she was doing this. Because she didn't need him to tell her that he wouldn't answer a call like this again. She knew it.

Theo shifted in his chair then, in a way that suggested he was preparing for a fight, those dark eyes seeming to laser into her. He seemed bigger, suddenly. Darker. "You're seeing me right now. Witness the glory of technology. And my surpassing joy."

"In person."

He laughed, a harsh scrape of sound that lodged in places it shouldn't. "No."

"Oh, I'm sorry." She smiled again, even more icily, because this was how she had to play this. No matter how tired she was of it or how sick it made her. "That wasn't a request. Did it sound like one?"

"It wouldn't matter if it was a formal summons from God himself," Theo remarked, almost idly, but she could see his expression and knew there wasn't anything idle about this man any longer. Had she done that, too? "The answer is still no."

"Theo." She shook her head as if he disappointed her, hiding her clenched hands in her lap, out of sight. "There's no reason we can't pretend to be civilized. Some things require a face-to-face meeting whether you want to admit it or not. You don't want to make me do this on a video call, do you?"

"It has been perfectly clear to me and to most of the world, I'd imagine, that I can't make you do anything," he replied in that lethally soft tone that sent spears of ice down the length of her spine and a hot curl of shame deep into her belly. "Certainly not behave as a wife should. You couldn't even manage to remain faithful to me for six short months. What, pray, could I possibly *make* you do now?"

Holly didn't flinch. How could she, when she'd told that lie to his face? Deliberately and with a full understanding of what would happen once she did? She was all too aware she'd brought this on herself.

"I want a divorce," she said now. Simply and distinctly.

As if it were true.

"My answer is the same as it has ever been," he replied in the same cool tone with all that rampaging fire beneath it. "You can't have one. Is that the reason for all this theater today? You could have spared us both. In future, I suggest you do."

"We don't have much of a future left, is the thing," she told him then, as his hand moved toward his screen again. Again, he stopped. When he only glared at her, she summoned that hard-edged smile again and aimed it at him as if this was all somehow amusing to her. As if she really was the woman she'd pretended to be these past four years. The woman, she knew, he fully believed she was. "I know that we've had fun these past few years—"

"Is that what they call it in Texas?" he asked, his voice even softer but no less vicious. "That is not the word I would choose for any of this."

"—playing all these games, scoring points, all this tug-of-war nonsense." She shrugged. "But all good things come to an end, I'm afraid."

"I'm not giving you a divorce, Holly. I don't care what argument you trot out. And, as I believe I've made perfectly clear with your generous monthly allowance and the life you live without any interference from me, I really don't care what you do. Or who."

"So you say," she murmured.

But she didn't believe him. She *couldn't* believe him. A harsh, predatory light flared in his eyes then, turning them volcanic with that edgy fury of his, making Holly's heart jolt and then catch inside her chest. Once again, she chose to call that *hope*.

"The only thing I will not give you is your freedom."

"And why is that?"

"Because it is the only thing I know you want, *agapi mou*," he said, his voice harsh and cold, especially when he called her *my love*. Holly couldn't let herself dwell on the way the endearment sounded now, when he didn't mean it at all. Not when she was sure they could both remember too well how he'd sounded when he'd meant it with every last shred of his heart, his soul. Not now, while he could watch her reactions. "Aside from my money, of course."

"Goodness," she drawled, and put a theatrical hand to her chest, because that was the best way to cover the sensation of it being ripped straight out from behind her ribs and then stamped on. She ought to be used to that by now, having done it herself the first time. "So possessive, Theo. Be still my heart. I'm tempted to believe you still have feelings for me."

"I don't." His voice was a growl. "I told you this four years ago, and I meant it. Spend my money. Embarrass me. I don't care. You can have anything you want except a divorce. That's not negotiable. If I have to live with this marriage, with the unfortunate choices of our tattered past, so do you."

"Except you've run out of time." She shrugged when his glare intensified. "That's Greek law, Theo." She made a show of picking up a piece of paper on her desk and reading from it, though she didn't have to read the words there. She knew them by heart. "Divorce is granted in cases of marital breakdown. And if the spouses have been separated for at least four years there is the presumption of that breakdown, regardless of whether or not you'd prefer to continue torturing me across whole decades."

"We are not separated. You left." His dark gaze licked over her, fire and fury, and what was wrong with her that she felt it echo within her—as if it was some kind of caress? "You can always return to me, if you are feeling unaccountably brave. Or foolish. I've told you this for years."

Dared her, more like. *Come back and face your sins*, he'd told her years ago, a dark and terrible promise of retribution in his low voice. *Who knows? Perhaps I am more merciful than I appear.*

But they both knew better than that.

"The four years is the sticking point, I'm afraid." Holly forced herself to hold that penetrating gaze of his, reminding herself that *this* was the easy part. That this would all be much, much harder if she got what she wanted and they did this face-to-face. If she'd been any good at dealing with this man in person, after all, if she'd been able to say what she felt instead of running away, none of this would have happened. "All I have to do is prove that we've been continuously apart for all that time, which we have and which has been exhaustively documented in at least three different tabloids, and then it won't matter what else happened between us…"

"If you spend your days telling yourself fairy tales about how you were the victim in this, I certainly can't stop you." His voice was made of granite then, and it landed on her, hard. "But on the occasions that you speak to me of our marriage, and I pray they remain rare, let's not hide in all the vague asides about 'what else happened.'" He leaned closer to the screen, his beautiful face harder than before, as if it was carved from the same stone as that harsh voice he used. "You happened. You are a liar. You deceived me from the start and then, when that was not enough for you, you slept with another man and threw it in my face. Then you left me under cover of night rather than deal with what you did, and you've trotted about the world happily spending my money ever since. I won't call you a whore, as I have some respect for the oldest profession in the world. At least it is an honest transaction. You are nothing like *honest*. You are far lower than any whore, Holly. And you offend me in every possible way."

And she merely smiled back at him, pretending that wasn't one mortal blow after another. Pretending she could block out the disgust in his voice, the contempt on his face. Telling herself this would all be worth it in the end, that there was no point defending herself until they were in the same room again. Until she could see if it was still the same—that brilliant, soaring *comet*. That wild joy that had nearly taken her out at the knees every time he'd looked at her, every time they'd touched. That beautiful thing that had terrified her so deeply and so profoundly she'd gone to such extraordinary lengths to escape it, fearing— *knowing*—it would swallow her whole.

"Noted," she said calmly, amazed that she could sound so unmoved by what he'd said, and look it, too, in that tiny little box in the corner of her own screen that showed her cool expression. She was amazed she wasn't shaking in reaction, more like, or falling to pieces—but she could do that later. When she was alone again, in this gray little prison she'd made for herself without him. When there was no one around to disbelieve everything she said, because there was never anyone around at all. "But you're not understanding me."

"I doubt I've ever understood you," he growled at her. "Why should that change in the course of one call I knew better than to take?"

"I'm filing for divorce, Theo," she told him evenly. "I will cite our estrangement as cause and I will further claim that you were the one who broke our vows." She shrugged when he muttered something filthy in Greek. "I will be believed, of course. You were a famous playboy who'd slept with most of Europe. I was an inexperienced country girl on her first holiday abroad, completely out of my depth with you."

He ran a hand over his face. "Clearly."

She ignored his caustic tone. "The choice is yours. If you meet with me the way I've asked you to do, I'll consider not taking a majority share of Tsoukatos Shipping in the divorce."

Holly had thought he was angry before. But the look he turned on her then was like lightning, electric and hair-raising, and she was suddenly very glad she was safe in Dallas, thousands of miles away from him and all the things that look of his could do.

Not that distance made her safe. Nothing could. Not when Theo looked at her like that. Not when he thought such things of her. But at least distance could minimize the damage.

Or so she hoped. The way she felt at the moment, it could go either way.

"Fine," he bit out after a long, simmering pause. It took everything Holly had to sit still, to keep her expression impassive, to keep up the sickening pretense. "You want to meet with me in person? I'll subject myself to it, though I should warn you, you may find this reunion significantly less pleasant than you imagine."

"Less pleasant than four years of insulting calls about credit card bills to remind me whose leash I'm on or today's charming philosophical exploration of the meaning of the word *whore*?" she asked drily, her impassive demeanor cracking more than she'd intended. She could feel the way her own eyes filled with a furious heat. Nothing so simple as tears, but telling all the same. "I find that hard to believe."

Something lit his gaze then, and she felt it like fingers down the length of her back, as if she'd unwittingly made herself his prey. *Whatever works*, she told herself resolutely. *Either you'll find a way back to him or you'll finally be free to move on with your life, such as it is. It doesn't matter how that happens, as long as one of them does.*

But of course it mattered. Nothing else mattered at all.

"I'll choose the venue," he continued, that odd tension in him making him seem bigger again, and far more dangerous.

"If you feel like that makes you in charge of this, then by all means," she began, deliberately patronizing him, purely because she knew it would get under his skin.

"Barcelona," he said softly, cutting her off. And something of what she felt must have showed on her face then, as surely as if he'd kicked her in the stomach. Because he had. And she could see by the glint in his dark eyes and the harsh curve of his mouth that he knew it. That she wasn't the only one who could play these nasty little games. "The Chatsfield Hotel in three days' time. I believe you know it well."

He knew she did. He'd taken her there four and a half years ago for the best month of their marriage. Of her entire life, before or since.

"You want to discuss our divorce in the same place we had our honeymoon?" she asked, stunned out of her usual careful iciness, too taken aback to guard her tone or her expression. And for a hectic moment, she didn't care what he saw. Their weeks in Barcelona were the last, best memories she had of those long-ago days with him. Of the only real happiness they'd ever had, she'd often thought, and she'd held on to the silly idea he'd felt the same. "Theo…"

"Barcelona in three days' time, Holly, or not at all," he said with evident satisfaction, and then he finally ended the call with a single harsh sweep of his hand.

Leaving Holly to sit and stew in the mess she'd made.

Again.

* * *

Theo strode into his suite at The Chatsfield, Barcelona, behind the efficient porter, frowning down at his mobile as he swept through his endless stream of messages and email, only to come to a swift stop when he recognized where he was.

He knew this suite. He'd spent an entire month here, and more than he cared to remember of that time without stepping outside. He knew every goddamned inch of it.

The same soaring ceilings. The same view over the fashionable Passeig de Gràcia, the Spanish answer to the Champs-Élysées, with the gleaming Mediterranean Sea in the distance. The same delicately luxurious furnishings that made the whole space sparkle with the restrained elegance The Chatsfield was known for all over the world. The small hallway adorned with bold local art leading to what he knew would be a master suite dominated by a wide, suggestive bed and a private balcony he'd used every last millimeter of back when. *Every single millimeter.* The same open lounge area scattered here and there with the same delicate rose petals that he remembered quite distinctly from four and a half years ago.

It was like stepping back in time. And he could hardly categorize the wild thing that surged in him then, chaotic and maddening. He only knew it nearly took him down to his knees.

This is unforgivable, he thought—but then, this was clearly Holly and her handiwork. There wasn't a single part of what she'd done to him in all these years that wasn't unforgivable. *Unforgivable is what she does.*

At moments like this he thought it was who she was.

Just like your father, said a small voice inside of him. *She doesn't care how much she hurts you. She doesn't care at all.*

"Is this the honeymoon suite?" he asked the porter. More brusquely than he'd intended, he realized when the poor man jerked to a stop as if Theo had slapped him across the face. Theo's hand tensed as if he really had.

"Yes, sir," the porter said. The man launched into a recitation of the room's many amenities and romantic flourishes, only to taper off into a strained silence when Theo merely stared back at him.

Theo eyed him for a moment, then turned his attention back to the room—and the low table before the arching windows that let the gleaming Barcelona lights inside, where a bottle of champagne chilled in a silver bucket. He didn't have to go over and look at it to know at once that it would be the very same vintage as the one he'd had waiting for them years ago. The one he'd poured all over Holly and then drank from her soft skin. From between her breasts, from the tender, shallow poetry of her navel. From the sweet cream heat between her legs he'd still believed, then, was only his.

Every last damned drop.

He thought for a moment that his temper might

black out the whole of the city, if not the entirety of the Iberian Peninsula, the shock of it was so intense.

"Thank you," he growled at the porter when he was sure he could speak without punching something, dismissing the man with a handful of euros.

Only then, only when he was alone, did Theo prowl over to the table and swipe up the card that sat there next to the silver bucket.

What a perfect place to begin our divorce at last, it read in Holly's distinctively loopy handwriting, as if she really was the madcap, innocent thing she'd fooled him into thinking she was when they'd met. *How clever of you to suggest it!*

And beneath it, she'd jotted down the mobile number that he'd committed to memory a long time ago, though he hadn't dialed it of his own volition in years. He was hardly aware of doing it now, but then it was ringing and then, worse, her husky voice was there on the line. And he was still standing by himself in a room where, the last time he'd been here, he'd thrust deep inside of her on every single available surface, again and again and again, because he hadn't known where he'd ended and she'd begun and it hadn't mattered. It had been pure joy.

Here, in this room, he'd truly believed he would spend the rest of his life enjoying that particular pleasure.

It was as if she'd catapulted him straight back into a prison built entirely out of his past illusions and he was certain she was well aware of it.

"How do you like your suite?" she asked as confirmation. Not that he needed any. And he supposed this was his fault for picking Barcelona in the first place.

"Come see for yourself," he suggested, and there was no hiding the fury in his voice. Or the other, darker things beneath. "You'll have to tell me if the furnishings are as you remember them. You were the one bent over most of them, as I recall, so you'd be the better judge."

Holly only laughed, and it wasn't that great big laugh of hers that he'd used to feel inside him as if he'd stuck his fingers deep in an electric socket. This was her *Holly Tsoukatos* laugh, more restrained and significantly less joyful, suitable for charity events and polite black-tie dinners.

Only a short, dull blade, then, as it cut into him.

"What a lovely invitation," she murmured. "I'll pass. But I'm down in the restaurant, if you'd like to come say a little hello. After all this time. As a casual introduction to our divorce proceedings. Who says we can't treat this like adults?"

"In public," he noted, and it took every bit of self-control he'd taught himself over these past years to tamp down on the roaring thing inside of him that already had him moving, as if the magnetic pull of her was too strong to resist. As if it had only ever been kilometers that separated them, nothing more. Nothing worse. "Do you think that's wise?"

Her laugh then was a throaty thing, and his hand clenched hard around his mobile even as every part of him tensed, because he remembered that sound too clearly. It dragged over him like a physical touch. Like her wicked fingers on his bare skin. He remembered her legs draped over his shoulders and her hands braced against these same windows as he'd ridden them both into wild oblivion. He remembered her laughing just like this.

He remembered too much. There were too many ghosts here, as if the walls themselves were soaked through with the happy memories he'd spent four years pretending had never happened.

"Nothing about us has ever been wise, Theo," Holly said then, and he blinked, because that sounded far too much like sadness in her voice—but that was impossible. That was the product of too many memories merging with the soft Spanish evening outside his windows, wrapping around and contorting itself into wishful thinking.

It took him long moments to realize she'd ended the call. And Theo stopped thinking. He simply moved.

He hardly saw the polished gold elevator that whisked him back down to the grand lobby. He barely noticed the hushed elegance, the well-dressed clientele, the tourists snapping photos of the marble floors and the inviting-looking bar, as he made his way toward the attached restaurant. Nor did he pause near the maître d'—he simply strode past the station in the entryway, his eyes scanning the room. An obviously awkward date, a boisterous family dinner. A collection of laughing older women, a set of weary-looking businessmen.

Until finally—*finally*—he saw her.

And that was when it occurred to him to stop. To think for a moment with his head, not the much louder part of him that was threatening to take him over the way it had the first time he'd looked up in a crowded place to see her sitting there, somehow radiant, as if light found her and clung to her of its own volition.

Before it was too late all over again.

Because she was so pretty. Still. Theo couldn't deny that and there was no particular reason that should have enraged him. And yet it did.

She looked smooth and edible in another one of those perfect little dresses that flattered her figure even as it made her look like a queen. Regal and cool and something like aristocratic, with her sweetly pointed chin propped in her delicate hand, her gaze focused out on the street beyond, and her other hand—the hand that still featured the two rings he'd put there himself, he noted, his temper beating in him like a very dark drum—toyed idly with the stem of her wineglass.

It reminded him—powerfully, almost painfully— of that too-bright afternoon on Santorini so many summers ago. He'd careened out of a strange woman's bed at noon and staggered out into the sunlight, as was typical for him. He hadn't headed to his family's villa for another lecture on his responsibilities from the exasperated father he'd stopped listening to years before, when the issue of the old man's character had been made abundantly clear. He'd walked up the hill to his favorite restaurant to charm the owner, one of his oldest friends, into plying him with good food to chase away the remains of another too-long, too-excessive night.

Instead, he'd found Holly, with her startled laughter and her bright, beckoning innocence, and his entire life had changed.

And she'd been sitting exactly like this.

Theo finally stopped moving then, right there in the busy aisle of the intimately lit restaurant, and forced himself to breathe. To *think*. To note that all of this was part of the little performance she was staging for his benefit—to achieve her own ends, at his continuing expense. She'd chosen to sit at one of the tables in the open windows over the busy, popular street, and Theo understood this was all part of her plan. Not simply to meet him in public, in a restaurant like their very first meeting a lifetime ago, but to do so while visible to the entire city of Barcelona, as if that might keep her safe.

She thought she was controlling this game. She thought she was controlling *him*.

It was in that moment that Theo decided to play. And to win.

He walked the rest of the way to her table and then slid into the seat across from her. He helped himself to her wine once he threw himself down, since they were dealing in echoes of the past. Why not do his part? He took a long pull from her glass, the way he would have back then, his mouth pressing against the small mark her glossy lips had left behind and then eyeing her over the rim.

He couldn't read her dark blue eyes tonight. He

couldn't see her every last thought on her face the way he could have back then. Then again, given the way she'd played him, perhaps he'd never seen what he thought he had. It didn't matter, he told himself then. This was a new game, and this time, he knew from the start that he was playing it.

There would be no surprises here. Not this time.

"*Kalispera*, Holly," he said, and when she blinked at him, he got the distinct impression she'd known he was there the whole time, despite the fact she'd been looking in the other direction. From the moment he'd entered the restaurant, even. He stretched out his legs and was instantly aware of how she shifted, to keep her own out of his reach, as if even that mild a touch might set them both on fire. She wasn't wrong and that, too, added fuel to the anger inside of him. And to his determination to win this thing, no matter the cost. "You look well enough. Spending my money clearly suits you. Is that polite enough to start?"

CHAPTER THREE

SHE'D DREAMED THIS a thousand times. More.

This is really happening, Holly told herself, trying to keep her expression blank. Or failing that, calm, which wasn't easy with the wild and erratic dance her heart was doing inside her chest. *This isn't one of those dreams.*

"Hello, Theo," she said calmly, as if this wasn't the first time they'd spoken face-to-face, in the actual flesh, *in touching distance*, in nearly four years. As if being back in Barcelona, at The Chatsfield of all places, meant nothing to her. As if she felt nothing at all—as if she really was the person she'd gone to such lengths to convince him she was. *Just a little bit longer*, she promised herself. "Did you have a pleasant flight?"

"Of course." He was so much *more* in person. She remembered the way his sheer presence had always seemed to scrape the air thin all around him, and it was worse now. As if he claimed more than his fair share of oxygen, simply because he could. Because he was Theo. "I do not maintain a private plane with my own staff for an unpleasant flight, do I?"

"I feel that way about closing down shops on Fifth Avenue and Rodeo Drive to make use of your black Amex card."

"So the dizzying bills remind me each time I see them."

His face was still so fascinating. Harsh and male and undeniably Greek, yet so intensely beautiful she wasn't surprised to see the way women and men alike reacted to him. The double takes. The second, longer glances. And none of them, she was sure, could see that ferocity in his dark eyes. The hint of violence she knew he'd never direct at her. Not physically, anyway, not in a way that would truly hurt her.

Sex, of course, was a different story—but she couldn't let herself think about that. About that last time, right after her "confession," so raw and possessive and *furious*...

"Is this small talk?" he asked softly. She wasn't fooled by that tone. She could feel its lethal power deep in her bones, tightening around her like a noose. "I haven't grown any more interested in such things, Holly. I told you four years ago what we would discuss if you dared face me again. Is this really where you'd like to have that conversation?"

"Far be it from me to direct you in anything," she replied, angling her body back so she looked far more at ease than she was, and it was harder than it should have been to remember what she was doing here, when he was *right there* and her instinct was to protect herself. To keep him hating her, which hurt more in the moment but was safer in the long run. Safer and colder and emptier. So much emptier. Hadn't she spent all these years proving that to herself—in case her childhood hadn't taught her that lesson first? "I know it's so important to you that you remain in control."

"I imagine that is the point of this charade, is it not?" He was stroking that wineglass the way he'd once stroked her body, and she was certain it was deliberate. That he knew exactly what that slow sweep of his tapered, too-strong fingers against the glass did inside of her. The streaks of fire. That deep, hard clench within. "The honeymoon suite, the clever little rose petals, like a forced death march down memory lane straight back into the fires of hell. And you have always done hell with such flair, have you not?" His gaze slammed into hers then. "What do you want from me?"

"I told you what I wanted."

It was hard to keep her voice even when he was on the other side of such a tiny little table, his intense physicality, his rampant maleness, like an industrial-force magnet. Holly had forgotten that, somehow. She'd forgotten that so much of being near Theo was being utterly helpless and under his spell. *In his thrall.* She'd had to leave him or disappear into him, never to be seen again, and she remembered why, now. She could feel it, like a black hole, sucking her in all over again—the same way this same kind of destructive love had sucked in her father all those years ago. She'd watched how this ended before. Why did she think it could be different now?

She kept her gaze level on Theo's and tried not to think about her parents. "A divorce."

"I told you I wouldn't give you one. And it has not yet been those magical four years that would release you, anyway. You shouldn't have come to Barcelona if that was really what you wanted. This resets the clock, does it not?"

"What does it matter if we're in the same city?" she asked, more bravado than anything else, and she threw in a little scoffing sound, just to maintain the brittle facade a few minutes more. "We're not staying together. We're not even staying in the same hotel."

That surprised him. Holly could see it in a brief flash of *something* before he shuttered that dark gaze of his, and that made her decision to stay in The Harrington, a luxurious boutique hotel in Barcelona's famous Gothic Quarter, seem that much smarter. As if she was getting good at handling him, after all.

After so many years apart, perhaps she'd finally learned something.

"I'll repeat—what do you want?" Theo's voice was clipped, his gaze when it met hers again uncompromisingly direct. "It was obviously important to you that we do this. Here we are. You have three seconds to tell me what your agenda is."

"Or what?"

Holly made her voice a taunt, though the truth was, she didn't recognize this version of Theo, and that was making her feel far more uneasy than she'd imagined she would. He wasn't the lazy, sun-drunk lover she remembered, and even though she'd read enough about him over the course of these past few years to have expected that on some level, the reality was much different. He had an edge now. He wasn't remotely tame. Back then, he'd reminded her of nothing so much as a great, lazy cat—tonight, he was all claws and fangs. Maybe that was why she was drawing this out instead of coming clean immediately.

Or maybe she was still too afraid. That he wouldn't believe her.

That he would.

"What can you possibly do to me that you haven't already done?" she asked instead.

"Excellent," he said silkily. "We've moved on to the blame portion of this conversation. And so quickly. Are you truly prepared to pretend that I carry any of it?" He laughed. It wasn't a nice sound. It rushed over her, making her skin prickle and feel too tight. It was as dangerous as he was. "I'll admit, I'm looking forward to the performance. Please, Holly. Tell me how *I* betrayed *you*."

She couldn't breathe. His gaze was too hot and too condemning, his mouth too grim. It was as if he'd chained her to her seat with the force of his fury alone, and she felt a dangerous weakness steal over her. As if she could simply surrender, right here…

But she knew better.

"I'm prepared to talk about our marriage," she said then, when she'd battled herself back from that cliff, down to something resembling calm. Or, at least, a good facsimile of it that might propel her through these last, crucial moments. "Are you? Because the way I remember it, the last time we broached the subject there was nothing but yelling and punching walls."

And then that wild, insane thing that had exploded between them, nothing as simple as mere sex—but she didn't say that. Neither did Theo. But it was between them all the same, the terrible heat and the violent blast of it as intense as if it had only just happened. That indelible claiming. Holly could hear the sound of his shirt tearing beneath her hands, could feel his skin beneath her teeth, the rage and the fire, the betrayal and the thick, twisted emotion like a hundred sobs pent up inside them both, and then that slick, perfect thrust of him deep into her, rough and complicated, their own painful little poetry. Their own goodbye.

"By all means, let's discuss our marriage." Theo shifted then, leaning forward, making the small table feel like a box, a cage—as if the restaurant all around them and the city just outside simply disappeared, folded into their past that neatly. When nothing between them had ever been neat. "Allow me to summarize the whole of it. I worshipped you. You betrayed me. The end."

"That's a bit simplistic, don't you think?"

"I find the truth always is." He didn't look entirely civilized then. Something raw and edgy stared out at her from his too-dark eyes, some kind of warning. *Or invitation*, a perverse part of her whispered. "And that's the story of our marriage, Holly. If you remember it differently, perhaps you have me confused with one of your other lovers."

"Have I graduated to *lovers*, then?" She'd meant to sound amused. Jaded. She missed both by miles, and he shook his head, as if he refused to let that sad tone of voice confuse him.

"I know you claimed there was only the one, but you'll understand, I think, if I find that difficult to believe. Given the circumstances. Who cheats only once?"

He said that as if he had dark personal experience with it—but Holly didn't want to think about that. Not now. Not when she was *this close* to telling the truth at last.

"Go on," she said quietly, straightening her shoulders and lifting her chin, as if he was pounding those hard fists into her. Some part of her almost wished he would. It would be more honest than the rest of this. More real. It might even hurt less. "Get it all out, Theo. All that poison. I know you've wanted this opportunity for years now."

"I have, in fact."

And Theo's smile was a blade that cut into her, deep. Not merely scarring her—it made her worry she would never be whole again.

But then, you're nothing resembling whole *now, are you?* asked that low voice she imagined was her father's, and she could only be grateful he hadn't lived to see what she'd made of her life without him—

though she thought he'd have understood. Perhaps too well. She was so much like him, after all.

"You dropped your bomb on me and were gone by morning," Theo said. "In time, I came to understand that this was all part of your grand plan. Moreover, that you always had a plan, right from the start. That I was nothing but a mark. The word that best fits, I think you'll find, is *mercenary*."

"I sound evil indeed."

Theo inclined his head. "Why discuss the details of your betrayal? It hardly mattered then, much less now. It was a means to an end, nothing more. I realized that what mattered to you was what you already had—my ring on your finger and access to my bank account."

"You could have come after me, if you were so desperate to talk," Holly pointed out.

On some level, she'd realized much later, she'd thought he would once the dizzy madness of their last encounter had faded. She'd had contingency plans in place to deal with him if he had. After all, he'd always pursued her so relentlessly before—wasn't that why she'd gone to these lengths to escape him? But he hadn't. He'd simply let her go. It had taken her a long time to accept that. Longer still to understand that as much as she'd wanted him to believe her when she'd lied to him, as much as she'd wanted to escape their all-consuming relationship, there was a part of her that had believed he'd see right through her. That he wouldn't let her do such a thing. That he'd known her better than she knew herself.

She'd twisted herself in so many knots that the only thing she'd known how to do was come back to him. "I told you I was going back to Texas. You always knew where I was."

He reached over and took her hand, and even though it was a cold little parody of the way he might have done it years before, that simple touch slammed through her. It wrecked her from the inside out, sparks cascading through her, her stomach twisting, her breath catching. If she hadn't been sitting down, she thought, she would have fallen over, and she knew there was no way he'd miss the way she trembled at his touch.

She hoped he'd think it was fear. Nerves. Not all of the rest of the things she knew it was.

Theo took the sapphire-and-diamond ring she wore—that he'd slid there himself, high on a Santorini cliffside as the wind toyed with her hair and the bright Greek sky kissed them with light—between his fingers and moved it gently this way and that, catching the candlelight and sending it dancing over the table, the way he'd always done in those first months, as if he was enchanted with it as she'd been.

Holly found she was holding her breath then. Waiting.

"That would have sent the wrong message," he said softly. So softly, it couldn't possibly be real. Holly braced herself, and his gaze moved up to meet hers with all that bright ferocity gleaming there, harsh and unmistakable. Pitiless. "I don't want you. I want the sweet, innocent girl I married, but she never existed.

Why would I chase after the deceitful little liar who pretended to be that girl? Why would I want you, whoever the hell you are?"

Holly pulled her hand from his, aware that he let her do it. His strength, his power, was like a bright light flooding through her. There was no mistaking it. There was no pretending he was anything but that ruthless, that damaging. Maybe he always had been. Maybe he'd hidden himself as much as she had.

"Is this where you doubt even the things you know were true?" she asked him, forgetting the mask she'd worn all these years, the game she was still meant to be playing. Forgetting herself.

"I take it you mean your convenient virginity, the great emblem of your trembling innocence." He lifted a shoulder and let it drop, and it was meant to hurt, she knew. It was meant to be dismissive and cruel. He was better at this than she was. "Yes, Holly. I have my doubts."

She couldn't pretend that was a surprise. Not really. And still, it made her feel empty. Broken and dirty.

"Congratulations," she said, aware she was giving him too much ammunition. Too much evidence to use against her. But she couldn't seem to stop herself. "You really have become your father. I should have taken the payoff he offered me."

He shifted, and she saw some dark thing move over his face, as if she'd scored a direct hit. But before she could tell him she regretted that, too, it was gone.

"I think we both know that a single lump sum

could never have satisfied you." He smirked at her, as if she'd imagined that darkness, and she was an idiot, wasn't she, to be at all surprised that he looked like a stranger then. Not that man she'd loved—and who'd loved her—at all. "What I can't understand is why you burned out so quickly. You had me completely fooled. Why not take it all the way? Why not make sure I was tied to you forever in the time-honored fashion? You must know I would never have abandoned my own child. That had you fallen pregnant I would have been forced to play these games with you forever."

It was a mark of how ill-suited she was to this game despite all these years of playing it, Holly thought then, that it had never occurred to her that he would honestly think she could do something like that. For a moment her head felt hollow and her ears rang, as if he really had hit her, after all. As if she was close to collapsing when she knew that, really, this had only just begun.

She swallowed and it hurt. And worse, he was watching.

"Your father asked me something similar," she reminded him, and his expression iced over. "Right before I tore up his check and threw it in his face. I know you remember that as well as I do. Back then, you were outraged."

She reached for her wine, more to have something to do than to drink it, but she welcomed the tart slide of liquid when she took a deep pull. It was better than remembering that blindingly sunny terrace with the sea at her feet, Theo's gruff and suspicious father, the things he'd said to her through Theo's younger brother's pointed and unfriendly translations, or the way she'd had to throw herself in front of Theo to keep him from taking a swing at his own family members. All of which she'd thought was worth it—then. Anything would have been worth it then, if it had meant she'd end up with Theo.

Better to pray for wisdom, baby girl, her father would have told her in his gruff, remote way. *Better for your soul than a wish granted.*

She wished he was still alive. She always would. Just as she wished she still didn't know what he'd meant by that. But then, life wasn't about what she wished, or what her lonely father had wished, either. They'd both learned that the hard way.

"Outrage fades," Theo was saying, his voice like cut glass, to match the winter she could see on his face. "Especially in the wake of four years of proof that my father was absolutely right about you."

"Back then, you thought he was more than half a thug," she pointed out. She nodded at him, at the crisp shirt he wore, the perfectly fitted jacket. "Now look at you. You might as well be another one of his goons."

She saw his temper dance along the edges of his body, all of those stark, male lines drawing taut and hard, and a hint of something much darker besides. But he only laughed again, and she knew it wasn't optimistic advertising or hopeful PR on the part of his family's company, which she could admit she'd monitored much too closely over the years. Theo really had become as formidable as his terrifying tycoon of a father. He'd become the Tsoukatos he'd always claimed wasn't in him.

"Is that meant to insult me?" Theo laughed again, though there was nothing like levity in the sound, or anywhere near those too-dark eyes of his. "I forget, you think you know me."

"I did know you, for a time." Holly had no idea why she said that. It couldn't help anything and, in fact, was likely to do nothing at all but infuriate him.

Which it did. She watched the storm break in his dark eyes, across his taut face, and felt it deep inside of her. That electric awareness—as if he'd changed the weather all around them.

"You knew a pathetic, weak creature who allowed a gold-digging tramp to walk all over him," Theo gritted out at her, every word like a lash. Like another blade, deep into her gut, and she'd brought this on herself, she knew. Maybe that was how she could survive it. "That man is dead. If in my resurrection I've become like the toughest man I know—the man who warned me away from a grasping American with dollar signs in her eyes, little though I listened to him when I should have done—I'll take that as a compliment."

"You can take it any way you like," she said, forgetting herself for another moment and letting too much emotion creep into her voice. She struggled to bring herself back under control. "It was an observation."

"Here's another one." He sat back, and it was a

confident victor's pose. It was the body language of
a man who thought he'd long since won the battle,
and Holly didn't like that at all. It made her shiver—
then, as quickly, fight to restrain it. "You no longer
have that power over me. I look at you and see nothing but an interchangeable blonde creature with too
much money and too little soul. There are hundreds
of women exactly like you. The only difference between you and the great sea of the rest of them is that
the money you spend is mine."

"You are a poet, Theo. Truly."

"You should have kept your distance." He shrugged
in that profoundly Greek way, though his dark eyes
glittered. "Here, now, I am bored. If you want a divorce, you're welcome to it. I have only one caveat."

"Of course you do."

"You must tell the truth." He smiled then, though it
came nowhere near his eyes. "I know that might prove
an obstacle for you, after all these years of games and
lies, but there it is. Simply admit your infidelity in
open court and we're done. It is as simple as that."

And this was it. This was the point of all of this,
because he was wrong. She did know him. Perhaps
not as well as she once had. But well enough to know
he didn't walk away from a challenge. She'd suspected he would do exactly this, hadn't she? It was
what she'd worked toward. It was why she'd wanted
to meet him in person to do this—though she would
never have picked Barcelona, of all the cities in the
world. Not the one place she'd held sacred between

them. But then, she supposed she should have anticipated that, too.

Because he would push the point. She'd known he would. Which meant she could finally tell him the truth.

There was no reason her throat should feel so dry. There was no reason she should feel that shaking thing deep inside of her, like a new kind of fear.

"And what if the truth isn't what you think it is, Theo?"

He sighed. "I don't care, so long as you tell it for a change. That is what I want. What I insist upon. Or I will keep you chained to my side like the family dog until you are so old you resemble that twisted, benighted soul inside of you." His dark gaze met hers, fierce and triumphant. "This I promise you."

She could still feel his hand against hers, his fingers on that ring he'd placed there himself four and a half years ago, as if he'd burned his touch deep into her flesh.

"I told a lie, yes," she said quietly. Why was this so hard? She'd practiced this. She'd imagined it a thousand times. Why did she feel as if his hand was wrapped around her throat, constricting her very air? "But not the one you think."

"Wonderful," he said caustically, his mouth flattening. "Did you sleep with the whole island, then? Not merely the one British tourist? I told you, I already suspected as much. I certainly don't need all the details now. Merely the admission in legal documents."

"I didn't sleep with anyone." She felt sick, somehow, as if she'd said too much, made herself too vulnerable in five little words. Or maybe it was that he'd know, now. The enormity of what she'd done. Of how far she'd been willing to go—and had gone—to escape him, and all the implications of that. "That was the lie."

Holly didn't know what she'd expected.

It had taken four years to say those words. Four years and a lot of time spent shifting through her motherless childhood and her father's take on that kind of loss, and thinking about how that had all led inexorably to the awful mess she'd made of both her and Theo's lives. She'd always imagined *something* would happen when she finally faced him again— because she'd known, hadn't she, that she'd never be able to look him in the eyes without telling him the truth. She'd barely survived telling him that huge lie when she'd done it initially four years ago.

Theo wasn't the only one who'd gone to great lengths to avoid this reunion.

She'd expected the world to stop spinning for a beat or two, perhaps. A moment of silence, of acknowledgment. Something—anything—to mark this literal moment of truth between them after all the darkness and misery of these past few years.

But the restaurant was cheerful and loud all around them, and Theo only rolled his dark eyes.

"I think we're going to need more wine," he muttered, and then he signaled the waiter, as if she hadn't said anything of importance.

Because, Holly realized then with an unpleasant shock, he didn't believe her.

It had never occurred to her that he wouldn't. He'd believed her instantly and completely when she'd told him that initial lie. He'd never doubted it for a moment since.

She didn't know if it was a laugh or a sob that escaped her lips then. "You don't believe me."

His own laugh was laced with pure derision.

"Why would I?" He rubbed one hand over his face, lingering on the dark shadow along his jaw that always turned up by the end of the day, and she could remember, in an unwelcome flash, the sweet scrape of it against the tender skin of her inner thighs. The perfection of that sting. "I'm not interested in all of these theatrics, Holly. Just tell me what you want and we can both go about our business. I've said you can have the divorce. I am nothing if not reasonable."

She couldn't breathe. She felt caught in him, trapped, as surely as if he held her in his own hands.

"And I suggest you take advantage of it," he murmured, that lash in his voice again. "I very much doubt it will last."

"I can't stand up in court and confess that I was unfaithful to you," she told him, and she knew he could hear the conviction in her voice. She saw the way his dark eyes narrowed, the way his sculpted shoulders shifted beneath his jacket. "Because I wasn't."

He sighed again, but there was speculation in his gaze, and something much hotter and much more dangerous.

"Then why would you claim you were? You were so certain, as I recall."

"I was insistent," she said, with more emotion in her voice—more temper, if she was honest—than she'd meant to show him. "*You* were certain. There's a difference."

"Such a tangled web, is it not?" he murmured, and he took the wine bottle from the waiter who brought it and waved him away, pouring his own drink. His voice was harsh when he continued, and mocking besides. "Tell me, *agapi mou*, why would you do such a terrible thing? Why would you tell your besotted husband such a hideous story, calculated to make yourself look so bad?"

"Because, Theo," Holly said, and there was no reason her pulse should be that loud, and so hard that she thought it might choke her. There was no reason that she should be *this* terrified of a little bit of honesty here and now, when she'd thrown herself headfirst into such a damaging lie four years ago. But it was only her voice that shook. Her gaze, at least, stayed steady on his. She told herself that had to mean something, to count for something. Surely. "I knew there was no other way you'd ever let me go."

CHAPTER FOUR

THEO LAUGHED THEN, and he could see the way she jerked in her seat, as if she could feel the darkness in that sound, the way it welled up within him and felt too much like poison. Like a deeply twisted need.

It was as if he'd touched her, though not particularly gently, and that fanged thing in him liked that a little too much. As if he really was—what had she called him?—a *goon*, after all.

As dark and as twisted as his own father.

"You were correct." He stood then, staring down at her, his usual fury mixing with something like pity, and he didn't know if it was for her or for him. He didn't know why he'd come here. Why he always acted first and thought second where this woman was concerned. Only that finally—*finally*—he was ready to end it. Once and for all. "But never fear, Holly. I have resigned myself to your absence. In fact, I prefer it. Allow me to demonstrate."

He expected her to follow him as he strode back out of the restaurant and she did, of course, catching up to him in the grand Chatsfield lobby. He heard the click of her heels against the marble floors and turned back when she was nearly upon him, letting his mouth curve into something even he could feel was vicious.

"How times change," he bit out as she rocked to a stop a little too close to him, a startled, wary sort of look on her face. "Now it's you chasing me across the world. Life is truly amazing, is it not? Its gifts never cease."

He watched her swallow, hard, but he couldn't read a single thing on her face. He told himself that was all the better. That he'd only ever imagined he could read anything in her in the first place. That it had all been a part of the games she'd played with him, games he'd lost spectacularly and no longer cared to indulge. Not after this latest bit of attempted deceit, to what end, he couldn't imagine.

"I had no idea you'd become so philosophical over the years," she said after a moment, in that too-calm voice of hers he'd already decided he hated, though he didn't care to explore his reasons for that. "I'm not sure it suits you."

He inclined his head. "I'll be certain to give your input the consideration it deserves."

They stared at each other, and the quietly exultant lobby seemed to fade around them. But the driving fury that had brought him here from Greece, the focused rage that had catapulted him from his suite down into the restaurant, had settled into something else. Something slick and hot that wound inside him and yet made him feel calmer than before. Different.

"Is this it?" he asked after a moment dragged by

and she only stared back at him. "This is why you insisted we meet? You wanted to tell me fairy tales about what you did four years ago?"

"It's true." Her voice was quiet, but he could hear the scrape in it. The hint of far darker, even painful, things beneath. "I spent a long time trying to un-ravel myself from you, Theo. I used every weapon I could think of, and then, at last, the only one I knew would work."

He wanted to shake her, and loathed himself for the urge. He was not that kind of man. He was no cave-dwelling animal. He hated that in her presence he needed to keep reminding himself of that.

"For future reference, may I suggest a simple state-ment of intent? 'I want to leave you, Theo,' you could have said. It's remarkable how a handful of words could have accomplished the same thing and with much less carrying-on."

"You weren't exactly easy to talk to," she grated at him, as if her throat was constricted. "Then or now."

"Ah, yes. I knew it must all be my fault, some-how." Theo all but bared his teeth at her. "I caused your infidelity, obviously. I forced you onto another man's penis."

He heard the breath she sucked in then, as if she was winded.

"I lied about that."

"Let's say, for the sake of argument, that I believe you," he said, leaning in closer to her, which was not smart. Or at all strategic. He could smell the scent of her skin, that hint of vanilla and spice, and it made him so hard it hurt. He ignored it. "What does it matter now?"

She jerked where she stood, tilting her head back to look up at him, and for a moment, she looked lost. She looked like the Holly he remembered—the Holly he'd created in his own head and knew better than to believe.

"What?"

This is her game, he roared at himself. *This is what she* does. *She is no more lost than you are.*

"It has been four years, Holly. What did you think this announcement of yours would accomplish?"

Again, that artless look of confusion that was truly masterful, he had to admit. It not only made him hunger for her as if he didn't know any better, it made him want to gather her close and protect her. She was frighteningly good at this.

She swallowed. "I just… I thought you should know."

"I see. How did you imagine this would play out? I wonder." He crowded her, moving until she had no choice but to back up, until he reached out and took her shoulders in his hands. He ignored the shock of it, the searing kick of sensation. Their chemistry wasn't the point here, and that startled glint of awareness in her gaze was likely feigned—because he knew better. *He did.* He learned from his mistakes, damn it. "Am I meant to fall to my knees? Sing hosannas? Jump up and down with joy?"

"Or, possibly, be slightly less aggressive and mocking," she retorted, her blue eyes flashing—though he imagined that was as much because he was touching her as because she'd found her tongue again. "To start."

Better not to think about her tongue.

"I don't believe a word you say," he told her then, crooning it to her, as if he was murmuring an endearment. "You showed me who you were when you left me, Holly. You've spent four years proving yourself to me, bill by bill. There is nothing on earth that can convince me this sudden about-face is anything but another act."

"That doesn't make what I told you any less true."

Theo laughed again and let go of her, watching her without any kind of pity when she stumbled back a step, then caught herself with a hand against one of the great pillars. A shaky hand, he noticed, and then promptly shoved aside.

His jaw felt like stone. "I hope, for your sake, that it is not."

She shook her head, as if she was dizzy.

"I don't understand," she said, but her voice was thick. She coughed to clear it. If this was real, if *she* was real, he'd have thought that was distress. But that wasn't possible. "Wouldn't you prefer that I made it up?"

He didn't mean to move but suddenly he was so close to her that he could see the panic and need on her face, the flush of color that told him too many things he had no intention of acting upon. Theo shoved his hands deep in his pockets to keep them off her, but he didn't back up. He liked that look of uncertainty on her face. He liked knowing that she had no idea what he'd do next.

Whatever else she might be faking, she couldn't fake this *thing* that still spiked the air between them. And he could use that as well as she could. Holly had made him feel powerless four years ago. She never would again. No one would.

"There is no doubt that you are a creature made entirely of deceit," he said softly. Lethally. "The only question is, what kind? Either you lied about who you were four and a half years ago when you vowed you could be faithful, or you've lied ever since. One makes you a con artist. The other makes you insane." He leaned in closer, putting his mouth to her ear and drinking in the faint tremors he could feel move through her body, telling himself he was the one manipulating her here, that he wasn't simply drawn to her again the way he always had been. "And I doubt very much a lunatic will manage to wrest a majority share of my family's company from an unsympathetic Greek court. If I were you, Holly, I'd stick to the tarting about and leave the supposed flashes of honesty to those who can pull it off."

But being close to her had its own perils, and he'd underestimated them, Theo discovered when he went to pull himself away. It was harder than it should have been. He was weaker than he liked.

He indulged himself instead. He propped one hand against the pillar beside her and angled his head closer, inhaling her scent. Letting it move through him, delectable memory and fresh need. Past and present. And then her hands came up—to push him away?—but she didn't. She only kept them there, hovering between them, as if she was more afraid to touch him than of what he might do.

Good, he thought. *She should be.*

"Efharisto," he muttered against the tender shell of her ear, keeping himself from tasting her the way he wanted to do by sheer force of will alone. "Truly, I thank you, Holly."

Then he pushed himself away from her and took a deep satisfaction in the way her chest rose and fell, as if she'd been running a race. Telling him everything he needed to know about that heat that still swirled between them. Telling him that keeping himself in check was worth the near-painful desire that raged in him now.

"For what?" Her voice was thick and flat and breathy at once and that, too, was a victory.

"For all of this." He thrust his hands back in his pockets. "For your lies, then and now. For playing your little games with honeymoon suites and your bouts of supposed conscience. You make this easy."

He turned and started not for the elevators but the front door.

"Where are you going?"

Theo had never pretended to be a good man, so he didn't waste time beating himself up for the dark thrill that moved in him then, at the confusion in her voice that even she couldn't feign so convincingly. He stopped and looked at her over his shoulder, framed by the marble pillar and the gleaming Chatsfield lobby all around her. She looked lost. Truly lost, this time. He liked it.

Hell, he reveled in it.

"Out."

"Out?" As if she didn't understand the word.

"I don't want to have a meal with you, Holly," he told her, and he made no attempt to temper the steel in his voice, or the harshness he could feel in his gaze, and he didn't care if every last person in the lobby overheard him. "I didn't want to have half a drink. You're only good for one thing, and the truth is, I have no idea where you've been, do I? I think I'll take my chances in the clubs instead."

She looked dazed. "But…"

"If you do the same, I'd suggest you dress less Manhattan cocktail party and more Ibiza party girl," he advised her silkily. "Or I doubt you'll attract the kind of tourist trade we both know you prefer."

"I want to make sure I'm understanding you." She was pale, and he liked that. He wanted this to hurt. He liked that it did. It felt like balance, after far too long. "I'm standing right here, I told you that our separation was based on an awful lie I told four years ago and you're leaving to go pick up other women at some nightclub."

And Theo smiled, enjoying himself for the first time since his secretary had marched into his office a few days ago with Holly on video, wrenching him back into their complicated and unwelcome past.

This part, he could do. This part, he was small and petty enough to revel in.

And it still wasn't the least of what she deserved from him. But he supposed he'd find a way to accept that, too, because he was finished with this. With her.

"I am," he said, making no attempt to keep that dark amusement from his voice, his face. "But no need to be so glum, Holly. I keep telling you. I don't give a toss what you do. You're welcome to come along and watch."

She stood there for a long time after he left, utterly frozen. Her back was pressed hard against the marble column and her heart seemed to slam back into her chest with every beat, and she couldn't catch her breath.

But he didn't come back. Just like four years ago, he hadn't come after her.

Holly supposed it shouldn't surprise her, but it did.

Theo had waited for her to respond and when she hadn't, when she'd only stared back at him in that same confused daze that had felt a great deal as if she'd turned to stone herself, his smile had deepened. And it had hurt much, much worse.

"Suit yourself," he'd said in that low voice of his, and then he'd laughed at her, mocking and horrible. Again.

And then he'd turned and walked away from her. Out into the street and the soft Spanish night.

It took Holly much longer than it should have to accept that he really, truly, had left her there. When she did, she told herself that what she felt then—that great heaviness plummeting through her and leaving deep, deep gashes as it careened off her insides—was anger. Righteous indignation. She'd spent all of this time feeling terrible for how she'd treated him when, in reality, he truly was the awful man so many of his business rivals liked to claim he was when he beat them.

But by the time she made it back to her hotel, the lovely Harrington in Barcelona's historic Gothic Quarter, she'd run out of ways to convince herself that she was angry at Theo. She was more angry with herself.

"What did you expect?" she asked herself as she walked toward the hotel's front door, not realizing she was speaking out loud until the doorman raised a quizzical brow at her. She smiled tightly and walked inside.

The Harrington was smaller than The Chatsfield, less like an opulent cathedral and more like an intimate and elegant little church, and yet she felt as graceless here as she had standing dumbly in The Chatsfield's lobby. She might have felt instantly comfortable in The Harrington when she'd checked in yesterday evening in a way she never had at the glamorous Chatsfield, not even years ago with Theo, but even so she'd been unable to get that damned honeymoon suite out of her head. She'd thought that was such a clever thing to do. A way to pretend she was keeping Theo on edge when, really, she'd hoped the leftover echoes of their time there might soften him.

But of course, like everything else, it had only made all of this worse.

And not only because even the thought of Theo in that suite again made all the memories of their month there together sweep over her, like a storm front coming in, fast and lethal and infinitely destructive. Making her ache, molten and needy and still so alone. After all these years, after plotting her way into the same room with him, after finally telling him the truth, she was still alone.

She didn't know what that great pressure was that threatened to explode inside of her then, right there in the hushed lobby of The Harrington, but she knew better than to let it take her over in a public place. Barcelona might have felt like a very long way away from Dallas or even Athens, but Holly knew that there was nowhere on earth truly safe from the paparazzi. Not when Theo was involved—and she still bore his name, didn't she? She'd insisted on it, telling herself it was another way to poke at him—but the truth seemed so obvious now. Obvious and pointless.

She'd kept his name because she hadn't wanted to let go of him.

His name doesn't make you his, that low voice inside reminded her, sounding so much like her father again that the great sobs inside almost flooded her where she stood in the bright lobby. *Never did. Only you can do that, baby girl, and you chose to play these running games instead.*

It only occurred to her now, standing in the wreckage of her marriage, that her father might have been addressing the detritus of his own when he'd said things like that. That he'd spent all those years when it was just the two of them talking to Holly's absent mother, not really to her.

She'd spent so much time alone and missing someone that really, she thought now, a little wildly, she should have been used to it. She should have been *good* at it.

Holly made her way up to her well-appointed and cozy suite and stripped off her clothes in the bedroom, throwing her dress across the four-poster bed and then yanking all the pins out of her hair, shaking her head until the heavy weight of it swirled all around her. And only then did she feel as if she'd caught her breath—and beaten back that terrible, jagged thing inside of her that still pressed too hard and threatened to swamp her entirely.

At least for the moment.

She checked the slim gold watch on her wrist and saw that it was a little before ten-thirty. She reminded herself that she was almost certainly jet-lagged, like every other time she'd ever taken the long flight to Europe from Texas, and she called down to the hotel kitchen for a late dinner. And blamed the events of the evening and her own outsize reaction to Theo to the time change and the wine she'd drunk while waiting for him to appear.

Tomorrow will feel better, she told herself fiercely, the way she had when she was a kid and she'd worked so hard to help her father save their battered old ranch, as little as it had been worth saving. The way she had when she'd been a teenager and had finally realized that her mother, who'd taken off with a minor rodeo star when Holly was six, had no intention of ever coming back or making things right. The way she had when she was older still and her father had been in the hospital, so frail and yet still so stubborn, and he'd refused to take the money she'd made.

The way she had in those early days after she'd left Greece and her marriage and Theo behind and had thought it might actually kill her, how much it hurt.

And if the next day hadn't actually been any better, well, eventually a day dawned that had been slightly more bearable. As far as Holly could tell so far, life was all about holding on until that next, nonterrible day, and sometimes that took a while.

Why should this be any different?

She ate the exquisite food they whisked up to her, seated out on her small balcony, in the midst of all the magic of a Barcelona night. The lights, the energy, which she could almost taste in the air around her. She closed her eyes and tipped her head back and let it all flow into her. Then, when she'd finished gorging herself on the local cuisine, she drew herself a bath in the luxurious, claw-footed tub and soaked herself until she was calm and shriveled in equal measure.

It was after midnight when Holly brushed out her hair, rubbed cream into her skin and then crawled into her bed, confident she'd drift off at once and sleep like a log until morning.

But instead she lay there, wide awake and scowling at her ceiling.

Theo was here. In this same city, right now.

Right now.

Out in one of the clubs, dripping with all of those beautiful Spanish women, and still as furious with her as he'd been four years ago.

She couldn't stand it.

Holly was up and out of the bed before she knew she meant to move. She ransacked the wardrobe she'd brought with her, pulling on a short skirt and pairing it with a pair of dramatic wedges that laced up around her calves and made her legs look edibly long, and then tossing on a filmy, slithery top she usually only wore to the beach. She raked her hands through her hair and let it turn into thick waves, added some drama and mystery to her eyes, and when she was done, she looked a great deal more like the half-gypsy traveler she'd been four and a half years ago than the elegant member of elite society she'd been pretending she was since.

She told herself that was merely a coincidence.

But deep inside, down low in her belly and lower still, where she was still nothing but a wild heat and all of it for Theo the way it always had been and always would be, she knew better.

She always knew better.

Holly found him in the third club she visited and, by then, it was well after two in the morning and Barcelona was only just getting started. This particular club was on a little stretch with several others down near the water. She'd peered into several of its scattered VIP rooms before she heard the unmistakable sound of his laughter from behind a group of scantily clad young girls, all dancing suggestively.

Or maybe she'd imagined it, she thought after a moment, looking around the moodily lit room and not seeing anything. Not seeing Theo. There were only beautiful people dancing another endless Spanish night away, carefree and heedless, and there was a part of her that didn't want to find Theo at all. A part of her that wanted nothing more than to melt into the driving, soaring music and let it carry her off to whatever place all these people inhabited with such apparent ease. Somewhere that hurt less. Somewhere that permitted nothing to matter at all save the music that ebbed and coaxed and slid all around them. Somewhere as effortlessly beautiful as they all were...

And then the small crowd in the VIP room shifted, and there he was.

Theo.

He was still wearing his dark suit and looked even better all these hours later, his hair disheveled and that lazy, indulgent look on his face that she remembered so well from Santorini. He stood with one perfect shoulder propped up against the wall, a small smile on his lush mouth as he watched a smoothly gorgeous brunette dance beckoningly before him.

The air between them was filled with sexual tension. It was hot, intimate.

It was Holly's nightmare, and she'd walked straight into it

And then he glanced up and saw her, that dark

gaze of his slamming into her, hard enough it nearly knocked her off her wedges.

He went still. His face changed from sexily amused to harsh and starkly furious in an instant, and Holly wanted to turn on her heel and run back across the city to the bed she never should have left in the first place. So she had no idea where she gathered up the courage to walk straight up to him instead. What demon it was that spurred her on.

Easy to be bold when there's nothing to lose, came her father's voice in her head, though if she was honest, he'd never quite taken his own advice.

"Looking for fresh meat?" Theo asked, hideously, when she drew near enough to hear him.

But Holly felt like drawing a little blood herself, and so she only laughed. She'd collect all the wounds he caused and count them later, she told herself, when she knew how this ended.

"You might have to update your definition of the word *whore*," she said, and smiled sweetly at the brunette when the girl launched herself at Theo and clung to his arm like some kind of barnacle. "Because I think you're the one who fits the bill, *mi querido esposo*."

That last, in what little Spanish she knew, for the benefit of the girl.

My dear husband.

CHAPTER FIVE

THE GIRL, PREDICTABLY, blanched and let go of Theo.

Theo only held Holly's gaze, his own dark and furious and lit with a kind of warning she had no intention of heeding. Barcelona had woven its way into her skin, she told herself, and she felt like the night itself, a little bit reckless and a little bit seductive, capable of anything.

And it didn't help that she'd seen that look on his face as he gazed at that other woman—that look he'd once told her was only hers. She wasn't the only one who had lied, she knew now, with the benefit of hindsight and a little more life experience. It was just that Theo's lies had been the typical kindnesses between lovers, little signs of respect threaded into promises of forever, while her lie had been the nuclear option. The escape hatch.

"If I am suddenly your husband," Theo said, that dark fury making his eyes gleam and his mouth a hard and beautiful line she longed to taste even now, God help her, "am I to assume that this wild-child outfit of yours is for my benefit? I am filled with nostalgia." He reached over and took a thick wave of her hair between two fingers and tugged on it gently, so gently. It echoed in her, hard, as if it was a touch against her skin. Or the thrust of his entry. "But, of course, your ability to dress in character rather proves my point, does it not?"

"I'm sorry," she said when he dropped the thick strands of her hair as if he'd only then realized he was touching her, and she didn't try very hard to inject anything actually apologetic into her voice. "Did I ruin your big night out with my inconvenient appearance?"

"My night? No." His voice was dark and it moved over her like the air around them, like the music. An insistent seduction that called to things in her she'd long since forgotten were there. "My life, on the other hand? Very likely."

"Everyone needs a talent," she replied, as if they were flirting with each other. As if there really was nothing in the world but the sneaky tilt and roll of the beat and that look on his face, so narrow and *intent*. "What's yours, Theo? Aside from talking every single woman in Europe into your bed, that is—which I thought you'd claimed you'd outgrown?"

"You must be kidding. Or you really are insane. Is that it?"

"It's okay." She tilted her chin up and only then realized she was too close to him and that the things that swirled inside of her weren't the music or the crowd or even adrenaline. It was all their history. It was the same old, incapacitating *need*, and tonight it made her as furious as he looked to be at the moment. She felt blind with it, ripe and near to bursting. "I'm sure that was one of the lies *you* told, that you've quite naturally overlooked in all your deep and abiding nasty judgments of me."

He let out a sound that was far too harsh to be a laugh, and then his hand was on her arm, and something in her thrilled to that no matter how dangerous it was. How out of control all of this was.

She didn't care that it wasn't a particularly kind touch, that he took her and then propelled her across the crowded space as if he might very well throw her out the door—and she let him because she couldn't seem to do anything but acquiesce when he touched her, as always. She didn't care that nothing good could come of this and that she really, truly, should have stayed locked away in her room at The Harrington, catching up on her sleep, the better to deal with him again come morning. Theo steered her into an alcove she wouldn't have known was there and didn't want to question why or how he did, pushing her inside and kicking the door shut behind him with a loud *thunk*.

They were up in a small glassed-in booth above the main dance floor, and it was heaving down there. Crowded and wild and somehow glorious in all its hedonistic excess. Holly could *feel* the bass thumping against the glass in front of her, taking over the kick of her heart and that pulsing thing between her legs, and then Theo was there, right there behind her, pressing against her back in a silent threat.

Or maybe this was merely a dark and heady sort of

promise, not a threat at all. Either way, she found she couldn't breathe. She didn't *want* to breathe.

"Is that why you came here?" he growled at her, into her, so it shook her the same way the deep roll of the bass moved the glass. Or maybe that was the hard expanse of his chest, his abdomen, pressed against the flimsy barrier of her light shirt, making her skin feel pink and hot beneath it. "Jealousy after all these years? Or did you want to take her place, perhaps?"

"I doubt you know her name."

"I knew yours. I gave you mine."

Another growl, and he was nothing but heat and strength, plastered hot against the length of her spine. His hands were at her sides, tracing her shape as if he still had that right, and Holly found her palms flat against the glass before her, as if she could hold on to that wild, seductive beat. Or to him. It all felt inevitable and reckless at once, and she couldn't seem to do what she knew she should, what self-preservation demanded she should.

The truth was, she didn't *want* to stop him.

"What good did that ever do?" Theo muttered.

And then his hot mouth was against the side of her neck, as insistent as the music, as delirious and as seductive, and Holly simply catapulted off the side of the earth the way she always had, every single time he'd touched her. Her body was still his, always and only his. It fell apart for him. *She* did, as easily as if it had been moments since he'd last had his talented, inventive hands on her instead of long, lonely years. Her breasts swelled and ached as his hands moved unerringly beneath her airy shirt, sleek against the skin of her belly, then moving up to hold them, her nipples hard points against his palms.

He left one hand there, teasing that jutting peak with casual mastery, torturing her sweetly, while his other hand traveled south. And all the while he tasted her, from that treacherous sweet spot behind her ear to her shoulder and back, and she did nothing but let him.

And exult in him. *Long* for him, as if there had never been anything between them but this. Simple and undeniable. Overwhelming and perfect.

The truth of them in that wild, impossible fire, scalding her, making her burn bright and hot and long.

"You are still so hot for me," he said at her ear as his hand slipped beneath her skirt and then held her heat in his hand, just held her there, completely his. Her back arched of its own accord, pressing her breast above and her core below deeper into his clever hands, her head falling back against his hard shoulder. "Will you be as wet as I remember, Holly? All these years later? As wild and ready for me no matter where or when or how?"

He didn't wait for her to answer. Did he know she couldn't speak? That her voice was lost somewhere in the music, the dark, the fiery spell he'd suspended them in? That all she could do was shake as he held her on that delicious edge?

She imagined he did. Of course he did.

Theo merely shifted and let his fingers stroke up under the edge of her panties, a teasing hint of wildfire, and then he thrust them deep—so deep, so perfectly deep—into her molten heat.

It was like bursting into flame. Like combusting. And he thrust again with his two fingers deep into her, that other hand hard against her nipple and his hot mouth on her neck, and it was as if that same comet she remembered so well streaked from the heavens straight into her.

And she came apart.

That easily and that disastrously, the way she always had. She bucked against him. She called out his name. She forgot herself completely. And when she went limp in his arms, he held her there, his big hand still cupping her heat and his fingers still deep within her, and waited for her to breathe again.

"You certainly seemed to enjoy that, Holly," he said, cool and harsh and directly into her ear so there could be no mistaking his bitter tone, the hard slice of it deep into her. "Is it the same for all your marks? Is it a game you play or are you truly that easy?"

She felt cold then, instantly, as she imagined was his intention. She shoved against him to get away, the shocking intensity of her climax shifting into a kind of suffocating horror that beat at her. And it was aimed mostly at herself, she knew. Holly felt herself tip over toward tears as she pulled her clothing back into place and turned to face him, that throbbing glass at her back. Theo dark and vengeful before her. Somehow, she blinked the tears away.

But she couldn't make Theo disappear that easily. Much less their past.

It was a very small alcove and he didn't move. He was too big and devastatingly lethal besides, and he merely watched her for a thundering sort of moment, then another, nothing the least bit soft or apologetic on his beautiful, stern face. Instead, he held her gaze as he raised his hand and licked her from his own fingers.

She shouldn't feel that like a shuddering heat. She should be appalled. She told herself she was, but nothing with Theo was that easy. Nothing ever had been, especially not her reaction to him. Her body didn't care what he said. It simply hungered for him the way it always had. Even more now.

"Stop it."

He ignored her.

"You still don't taste like the liar we both know you are," he told her, deliberate and even, his dark gaze never wavering and that gleaming, furious thing keeping her frozen where she stood, as if he'd nailed her feet to the floor. "It's like magic."

"I told you," she managed to say, over that pounding, jolting thing inside her chest she understood was her heart, "I never cheated on you. Never. I lied about taking a lover. What will it take to prove that to you?"

He rolled his eyes and that was too much. That and the fire she could still feel inside of her, charring her, changing her. She felt the tears spill over and hated herself for that. She felt raw and broken, and the worst part was, she could still feel his touch, could still feel the leftover sensation as if he'd branded her somehow with his hands and his mouth. As if a single climax could never be enough to soothe this hunger for him.

Nothing had ever been enough. That had been the problem.

"I'm telling you the truth!" she hurled at him.

She could feel the blast of his temper, a thick, black thing, though he didn't move a muscle. Then he did, and she heard herself make a small little noise of panic or longing or both when he moved toward her, taking her chin in his hand and pulling her face toward his, close enough to kiss.

Though she knew, somehow, that kissing her was the last thing he was about to do.

"I believed you, Holly," he grated at her, and his fury was different, suddenly. It looked a little too much like grief. It scared her. "Back then. And why, I asked myself, should I hold my wedding vows sacred when you had profaned them as many times as you could? No doubt far more than you'd dared admit?"

"I'm trying to tell you, I didn't…"

"I hope this is nothing more than another one of those sick games of yours that no one ever wins." His voice was a thing of stone, a monolith, and it crushed her. "Because know this. Once you revealed yourself to be faithless, I saw no reason to adhere to the very vows you'd thrown in my face."

She didn't want to understand him. She refused to let herself, no matter that harsh cast to his mouth, the too-still way he stood. She told herself he was the one who wasn't comprehending her, even as something devastatingly icy began to emanate from inside of her. From every place he'd touched her.

From that suddenly hollow place inside her chest.

"Theo." She was whispering. "I never broke our vows. Not like that."

His dark gaze went bleak, then uncompromising. It was so black it hurt.

But he didn't look away. If anything, he stood taller. "But unfortunately, Holly, I didn't know that. So I did."

When she shoved past him, hurtling herself back through the door and out into the crowd again, Theo let her go.

He told himself he *wanted* her to go, and he did. Of course he did. He hadn't wanted to see her again in the first place—this had all been her idea, her threat, her execution. Let her run away. Let her do whatever the hell she wanted. Let her disappear back into the club, back into her new, separate life that he refused to believe had really been some exercise in born-again chastity the same way he would not accept that she'd lied back on the island four years ago. Let her go right back wherever the hell she'd come from this time with her new set of painful, damaging falsehoods and her big, soft, hurt eyes he couldn't seem to get out of his head.

Those eyes. Like broken blue. And this time, he'd done the breaking.

There was no earthly reason he should believe her, he reminded himself as he scowled down at the main dance floor but saw only Holly's twisted face and her tears making tracks down her cheeks. This entire night was a show she'd decided to stage for her own reasons, nothing more, complete with the flower petals on the floor of his suite and that ridiculous see-through thing she'd worn here tonight that had made him nothing short of murderous the moment he'd seen it. It was another taste of her brand of marital theater and he didn't believe a word of it, anyway. Not one damned word that passed those deceitful lips of hers.

But her taste was in his mouth, sweet and as intoxicating as ever. It felt as if there was some kind of great stone pressing down into him where he stood, and he told himself he didn't want to know what it was or why.

Theo understood that he'd miscalculated. It wasn't a pleasant feeling. He should never have touched her. He should never have allowed himself to relearn the fact that the memory of her was but a pale and boring substitute for the real thing. Her sweet, hot, yielding flesh. The scent of her, soft and female, spice and sweet at once. The cries she made as she came apart in his hand.

Theo muttered something vicious and crude in Greek, then he slammed his fist against the wall of the alcove. *Once.*

He thought of her bright eyes, flooded with those tears that had to be fake but certainly hadn't looked it. That stricken, horrified look on her face he'd have thought couldn't be feigned, not even by an actress as accomplished as she was. *Twice.*

"Vlakas," he growled at himself because he was a stupid bastard, always and ever where this woman was concerned, and then he went after her.

He told himself it was self-preservation, nothing else. He convinced himself of that as he pushed his way through the oblivious crowd and out into the street, the soft Spanish air feeling thick around him, an unwelcome echo of her body slumped against his. It wouldn't do to let his errant wife career off into danger after an emotional scene with him—how would that look in the tabloids? As long as she bore his name, he lectured himself, she remained his responsibility.

He'd practically gone over all pious—not the best fit for a man of his nature, he could admit—when he caught a movement down the street out of the corner of his eye. A suggestion of the curve of her hip, a mere hint of her usual sweet gait that he would know anywhere, moving from beneath the street lamps into the beckoning shadows.

Theo caught up to her as she started toward the sand, as if headed for the dark waters of the bay beyond.

"Holly, stop," he ordered her as he came up behind her, and something seemed to ripple over her at the sound of his voice. In him, too, but he ignored that part.

He had no choice but to ignore it. It was that or go mad.

Holly's head was bent, her hair a wild mess around her shoulders in a way he hadn't seen in years, and

Theo was so caught by the thick fall of it that he almost missed the way her hands were clenched into tight balls at her sides. But she stopped walking and then stood there swaying slightly, almost as if she really was that obedient, and Theo couldn't tell which one of them he hated more in that instant. Holly for causing this mess in the first place. Or himself, as ever, for remaining so damned susceptible to her. Even now. Even on a dark street in Barcelona, where he still didn't know what to believe.

Much less how to feel. He thrust that aside—because he was very much afraid he knew how he felt and he refused, he damn well *refused*, to indulge it.

"Are you planning to fling yourself into the sea?" He sounded flippant and aggressive at once, but he couldn't seem to stop himself. His hand ached faintly from its hard contact with the wall in the club and he refused to look too closely at the things ricocheting through him, at the things it might mean if she'd actually told him the truth, for a change. If she really, truly, hadn't betrayed him four years ago—at least, not with her body. "That seems unduly histrionic. The papers would have a field day."

"What do you care?" she asked, her voice thick, as if she'd been screaming into the night before he'd found her, and he filled up with a dangerous kind of rage at the idea that he'd somehow caused *her* pain.

As if she had any right to feel anything here.

He wanted to poke at her until she made sense to him again, until she dropped this latest act and returned to form. He wanted to *reveal* her, somehow, on this dark side street mere steps from all of Barcelona's late-night club magic. Yet all he could seem to summon was a casual cruelty that did nothing to take the taste of her away and even less to move that great, hulking stone of a thing he could still feel pressing down on him, crushing him.

God, he hated this. He'd felt indifferent for a few moments back in The Chatsfield's lobby, and that had felt like a relief. Like freedom. Like some kind of resurrection, but it hadn't lasted. He'd already been bored and furious again when he'd looked up and seen Holly standing there in that VIP room. *This* was nothing new, this cut-to-shreds, dark and tormented *thing* in him. But he hated it all the same.

And then she turned around to face him, and the world seemed to slip a bit beneath his feet, rocking him. She looked wrecked. Utterly destroyed. And Theo felt perilously uneven, suddenly, scraped raw and hollow, because he knew exactly what she was feeling. He'd *felt* exactly what she was feeling.

He could see it right there on her face and she, by God, didn't deserve to feel that way.

"Don't you dare look at me like that." There was nothing flippant about him then. It was all aggression, all fury, and he made no attempt to soften it. He could feel it surging in him, making him feel something a good deal like drunk. "You did this, Holly. Not me."

He refused to feel guilt. *He refused.* But he understood that the thing that pressed into him was that, and more. Much more and much worse besides, and his refusal didn't seem to matter much. It was dark and fetid and it wasn't listening to him, a terrible coil of bitterness and regret and loss, and her taste in his mouth only made it worse.

And he still couldn't seem to find his feet beneath him.

"You win again, Theo." She sounded different. Not the cool, brittle queen of the charity circuit. Not the open and too-bright girl he'd married. *Weary*, he might have said. *Broken, finally.* "You've hurt me worse, at last. Hooray. Do you want me to congratulate you?"

"What did you think would happen?" He blazed it at her, and he didn't care, for the first time in years, if anyone was watching. Listening. He didn't concern himself with whether or not this entire conversation would show up on the front page of some sleazy tabloid and reveal all of their dirty laundry to the world. He didn't care about anything but shifting that *thing* off him, because he refused to accept that it was guilt. He refused to let it in.

That would mean believing her.

"I haven't accused you of anything, Theo." But her words were like bullets and he felt them punch into him, piercing his skin and burrowing deep. "I haven't called you a whore or myself a mark. I haven't said a damned thing."

He refused to believe her. This was just another one of her games, surely. *Then why are you out here, arguing about it?* a small voice asked reasonably enough inside of him. *If you really believed this was another lie, why would you care enough to follow her here?*

Theo scowled at her as if she'd been the one to say it. "If the sanctity of our marriage vows was important to you, perhaps you shouldn't have gone to such lengths to convince me otherwise."

"What lengths are you talking about?" she demanded, surprising him with the flash of temper in her eyes, the crack of it in her voice. "I said I'd done it and you believed me instantly. *Instantly.* You took no convincing at all. It was almost as if my betrayal was a foregone conclusion."

"Ah, yes. Revisionist history. My favorite."

She ignored his harsh tone, though her triangular chin edged up a notch, and that same temper flashed again, brighter, in her pretty gaze.

"I was a virgin when I met you. I'd managed to make it more than twenty years without sleeping with anyone but you. Yet you found it perfectly reasonable that six months later I'd had a blistering one-night stand with someone else whose name I didn't even bother to learn."

"Because you told me you had," he bit out, that heaviness inside him starting to spread out wider, press down harder, and he wouldn't let it. *He wouldn't.* "I wasn't some jealous maniac, bristling with accusations every time you walked down a street. It never would have occurred to me that you'd cheat on me."

"I know." Her voice was a terrible thing then, judgment and pain and something he didn't want to recognize, but the look in her blue eyes was worse. Much worse. "Because you and I were inseparable and in love and we spent most of our time in bed. Still, you believed, without question and despite everything you knew about me, that I had the time and the energy to nip down to a tourist bar and have a quickie in an alleyway with some stranger."

"Because you told me you had."

He didn't recognize his own voice and she shook as if it had been a roll of thunder instead, and he couldn't tell which one of them was the storm or where it was coming from, only that he had no idea how to escape it.

"I must be the world's best liar," she whispered, and her eyes were nearly black with torment. *Torment*, damn her, and there was no escaping that heavy weight then. It crushed him. It *flattened* him. "To fool a man as jaded and cynical as you were when I met you. Then again, perhaps you wanted to believe the worst of me. Perhaps that was what made it so easy to convince you." She laughed, and it made everything worse. "Believe I'm a whore and what does it matter if you are, too? You get to slip back into your old ways without a second thought."

"Don't you put this on me," he grated at her, scarcely aware that he'd moved toward her, or that his hands were on her shoulders again, pulling her up on her toes and much closer to him than was wise, so that her warm vanilla and faintly spicy scent surrounded him. "You lied to me of your own volition, Holly. Was there a gun to your head? Was there force involved? Was there some villain lurking in the shadows who forced you to ruin our marriage and run?"

"No villain," she threw back at him. "Just a husband who couldn't wait to get his own back."

She shrugged out of his hold and he let her go because that was the smarter course, not because he wanted to do it. His palms felt burned by the heat of her soft skin even after she moved. She staggered back a step, looking faintly dazed. Then her blue eyes narrowed on him.

"How long did you wait to start sleeping around again, out of curiosity?" she asked, her voice as crisp as her gaze was wild. "Five minutes? Or did you wait a whole night after I left, out of respect?"

CHAPTER SIX

"I LOVED YOU," he seethed at her, refusing to answer her, because this was the crux of it. This was the point, and she was twisting it and distorting him in the process. "And you destroyed me."

"If only that were true, Theo," Holly whispered, and he didn't know which she meant, that he'd loved her or that she'd destroyed him. Both. "But that was just what we told ourselves, wasn't it? I'd have to have really known you first, and you me." She made a hollow sort of noise. "And I think we both know that never happened."

She staggered back a step, then another, wrapping her arms around herself as if she was cold when the air was warm all around them. And somehow all of that black and terrible fury simply drained from him then. Not gone, he thought as he eyed her, but banked. He felt nothing so much as tired, and as ruined as he'd felt four years ago when he'd believed she'd betrayed him.

And worse than all of that, sad.

It was then he understood that he did, in fact, believe her now. Despite what that made him. Despite all the things that made him, that he'd promised himself he'd never become. Theo shoved a hand through his hair and tried to force air into his lungs, and Holly took another step away from him, looking over her shoulder toward the lights of the city, as if she could will herself somewhere, anywhere, else.

Anywhere but here, stuck in this misery they'd made, and for the life of him, Theo still didn't know why.

"Will you run now?" he asked her, his voice as soft as the night, and as dark. Inky and lethal.

"I…" But she didn't finish.

So Theo did.

"That is what you do, is it not?" He didn't sound like himself. But then, he wasn't *himself*, was he? He was the creature she'd made him. A man like his own father, the kind of man who lined up the promises he made in whatever shifting order of importance he chose and then ignored the rest when they became inconvenient. His own worst nightmare, in other words. He focused on Holly instead. "When it is hard, when it is intense, you make excuses or you lie, and then you run, and you leave nothing but this wreckage behind you." He shrugged. "Why should this be any different?"

That last part was almost the worst. *Almost.*

Holly felt half-dead   or maybe she only wished she did. Maybe she only *wished* she could retreat into something that much like oblivion, because that would make this easier, surely.

"I'm not running anywhere," she told him fiercely. But she had to lock her knees to keep from moving back even farther, away from that look on his face, anywhere at all but here with him. And she hated the fact that he could read her so well when it turned out she'd been so terribly wrong about him. It made her feel vulnerable.

Or *more* vulnerable, anyway.

And for what felt like forever, they simply stood there. The music from the clubs behind them was a wild smear of sound through the darkness, bass and drum and eerie melodies distorted by the water. And there was nothing but the sea in front of them, and yet they stood there as if they were on opposite sides of it.

"How many?" Holly asked. It was sick. She knew that. But she couldn't seem to help herself. And she couldn't seem to stop, either. "How many women did you sleep with? How many times did you pay me back for my betrayal?"

"I'm not going to answer that." His voice was a dark throb into the night, and she didn't know how he could do that—how he could sound so danger-ous and furious and lofty at once. "You do not get to claim any moral high ground in this, Holly. You are not the wronged party."

"But I am the faithful party, it turns out."

He let out a low, male growl that moved inside of her, half heat and half accusation.

"You cannot have it both ways. You left me. You

threw your affair in my face whether it was true or not, and then you left. That is not faithful, by any definition."

"How about the definition that involves sex with other people? How am I doing with that one, Theo?"

He shifted, and she had the impression he was holding himself back, but barely.

"What did you think would happen? Was I meant to suspend myself in pointless sainthood, awaiting this moment I had no reason to believe would ever come?" He let out a scrape of something too painful to be laughter, and it made Holly feel hollow and ruined at once. "You cannot be so naive."

She understood she wasn't being fair. That none of this was fair and that, worse, she'd put all of this in motion herself when she'd told that first lie. But she couldn't seem to stop herself.

"You never wanted a divorce," she said helplessly after a moment, when the buzzing in her ears stopped making her feel dizzy. "I suppose I thought…"

She shouldn't have said that, and Holly wasn't surprised when he seemed to rebound into a greater rage right there before her, his dark face taut and furious, his eyes blazing.

"That this was some kind of sick flirtation across whole years?" His voice was scathing. "That even though I believed that you'd cuckolded me, I still hoped to win you back with open access to my bank account and my otherwise complete and total indifference?"

"You're the one who taught me how to play these

games, Theo!" she hurled at him wildly, and she didn't have it in her to worry about what was *fair*. Maybe it was that word he'd used: *indifference*. Because that was what she'd seen in the lobby of The Chatsfield, and that was the end of everything. She knew that. "You could have come after me but you chose to throw money at me instead. Don't you dare stand here and accuse me of ruining our marriage when you did nothing to save it. When you no doubt rejoiced the moment I left!"

"Enough."

She'd never heard that tone from him before. Abrupt and powerful, reminding her who he'd become in these past years. The heights he'd climbed in his father's company and how like the old man he'd become along the way. It was only then she realized she was shaking again, and not from the temperature. She rubbed her hands up and down her own arms and his mouth tightened.

"Theo…"

But Holly didn't know what she meant to say and it didn't matter, because he was already shaking his head.

"I said enough." He closed the distance between them and took hold of her arm, and she automatically pulled against it, letting out a surprised sort of sound when his fingers only tightened. "Walk or be dragged, *agapi mou*." It was nearly a snarl, and she felt it like a slap. Or perhaps a kick. "In the mood I am in right now, I do not much care which."

Holly walked.

Theo kept a tight hold of her, and she told herself it didn't matter. It didn't make a difference that he had put those beautiful, gorgeous hands of his on countless other women, possibly even tonight before she'd found him. That he knew about places like that alcove because he'd used them, obviously, and not only with her.

That made her feel sick, it was true. And yet the pit in her stomach that yawned open wider with every step wasn't about that, not really.

This was her fault. No matter what she threw at him, she knew that. She had done this, no one else. She had remembered so vividly what her mother's departure had done to her father, how it had broken him but made him unwilling to go after her in all the years that followed out on that lonely little ranch, and she'd used it. She'd claimed the same sin and gotten the same reaction in response. *She'd done this.*

But knowing that only seemed to make things worse. Or maybe it just made her hate herself. She could hardly tell the difference any longer, and his fingers wrapped tight around her upper arm didn't help.

"I can take a taxi," she told him when she realized Theo was striding toward his car and the uniformed driver who beckoned from a spot down the street, but nearly swallowed her own tongue when he turned a savage glare upon her.

It seemed smarter to get in the car. And then to tell his driver where she was staying when asked, because that would be faster than fighting about it or trying to conceal it.

"Theo," she started again when the car glided into traffic, "I want to try to…"

"My mother died when I was only twelve," he told her in that abrupt way that made her think of that look he'd turned on her, cutting her off.

He sat beside her but he might have been worlds away, that fine body of his taut and visibly furious beneath his elegant clothes, his elbow propped up against the far window. He stared out of it, out toward the delirious explosion of the city and all its fantastical structures as if she wasn't there. But Holly didn't make the mistake of thinking he was speaking to himself.

"I know," she said quietly. "I'm sorry."

"It is the proper thing to murmur, as if it was a tragedy, or a mistake, but the truth is that she took too many pills with far too much alcohol and I believe it must have been a great relief to her to finally slip off into eternity."

Holly felt ripped wide-open. "I had no idea."

"My father told everyone she had lost a struggle with a sudden and violent illness, and I suppose, in some way, this is also the truth," Theo said in that same low, pointed way, as if he could have been talking of his shipping concerns as easily as these private family things Holly had never heard even a whisper of before.

He paused for so long she thought he was finished, and wondered why she trembled, why even her bones seemed to shake, but then he turned his head to look at her instead and it pinned her to her seat.

"But another, more pertinent truth is that my father's affairs were not only legion but common knowledge. Every piece of jewelry he gave my mother was a bribe, an apology, another young woman's body he'd taken as his due. This broke her, jewel by jewel and lover by lover, and he knew it. But he never stopped. And she draped herself in each and every one of them, every bauble that proclaimed my father's guilt and carelessness, when she killed herself to escape his endless stream of betrayals."

Holly couldn't move. The city lights played over her face, bathing them both in intermittent light as the car navigated the streets, but all she could see was Theo and that terrible gleam in his dark gaze, that grim line of his mouth.

She whispered his name, or she thought she did, and he ignored it, anyway.

"And tonight," he said quietly, with ferocious precision, "you have made me exactly like him."

Holly couldn't breathe. "I thought you admired him now. I thought everything had changed between you."

Theo's teeth bared in something far too stark to be a smile, and she knew he could see exactly what kind of coward she was, to avoid the point of what he'd told her. But she could hardly take it in. She wasn't sure she could bear it.

"I said he was a tough man. An excellent businessman." Theo's dark gaze hurt as it moved over her,

Holly realized. She was half-afraid it would leave scars, to fit right in with all the rest she bore from their time together. Not to mention the ones she'd caused. "I never said he was a good one."

And they sat in strained silence, another wound that would leave its mark, for the remainder of the ride.

"I will walk you to your door," he told her in that harsh way of his when the car pulled up to the tall, gleaming doors of The Harrington, towering over the narrow, medieval street. He didn't glance at her as he said it.

Holly swallowed, hard. "I can't think of anything less necessary than that."

She could simply go back to Dallas and resume her lonely, gray life, she thought. This was a terrible mistake, that much was clear, but she could remedy it. She could take the first flight out in the morning. She could stop playing stupid games with his money, her silly and childish attempts to gain his attention, and move on with her life, such as it was. All she had to do was leave.

"I didn't ask you for your permission, Holly."

"Why not pretend none of this ever happened?" she suggested, ignoring his tone and pretending that everything else that had gone on tonight wasn't crowding out her ability to think clearly. "We'll divorce and go on our merry way. We can start by you *not* walking me inside like this is some sick parody of a good date."

"You came on my hand not an hour ago," Theo

retorted icily, and turned that too-black gaze on her again, making her feel still and small. "Yet an escort to your hotel room is an intimacy too far?"

She didn't respond to that. She didn't trust herself. Holly climbed from the car and let him accompany her in a grim march across the lobby—though she wasn't certain *let* was the right word. How could she have stopped him? How could she have stopped any of this? Once she'd decided to leave him four years ago, had all of this darkness and despair been inevitable?

It made her feel something like seasick to think so.

They didn't speak on the endless, deeply fraught ride in the paneled elevator, nor the long walk down the hushed corridor to her room. She glanced at him when she went to swipe her key card, but he only stared back at her, stone-faced, with that vengeful glitter in his dark gaze and his hands thrust deep into his pockets.

"Open the damned door," he said when she paused, his voice soft but like nails even so. "I will not discuss any more of my private life in these open public places, filled as they are with so many eyes and ears."

A thousand hurtful replies to that swirled inside her then, but his glare only intensified.

"Don't push me, Holly," he advised her in that same tone. "Not tonight."

She opened the door and it felt like the worst kind of capitulation, but she wasn't sure she knew herself anymore. She felt like a marionette. As if her limbs were responding to some far-off controller and she could only do as she was bid.

Then again, maybe that was one more way to avoid taking responsibility for the mess she'd made of her marriage.

And then they were standing there in her hotel suite, which had felt comfortably spacious while she'd been in it alone. But Theo roaming through it, looking angry and male and *too much* in the midst of so much quietly assured elegance, made her feel trapped. Or perhaps that was the sudden lump in her throat, restricting her breath.

The insistent pulse of her own shame, her own deepening guilt.

Tonight you have made me exactly like him.

"I'm sorry," she forced herself to say, though she felt nothing so easy or uncomplicated as *sorry*. "I realize you acted only on the information you had. I have no right to blame you for that. I have no right to be hurt by what you did."

He'd moved over to the windows and he turned back then, something terrible on his face, caught there in his dark eyes.

"I cannot process this," he told her after a moment. "I cannot make sense of it. You have not only done a monstrous thing to me, to us—you made me into the very creature I vowed I would never become. I could not bear the first betrayal, Holly. I have no idea how I am to come to terms with this one, the one that makes me worse than you by any emotional arithmetic."

Her hands were in fists again, tight and hard against her thighs. "Is that what this is about? Who's worse?"

"I have no idea what this is about." His voice was harsh. "I cannot imagine you do, either, or it would not be this convoluted."

Everything had shifted. The room was so bright where the night and the club had been so dark, and Holly couldn't ever remember feeling so naked before. So wide-open and on display. She wasn't shaking any longer, but she felt even more broken than before, and looking at Theo made it that much worse.

He held her gaze from across the room, across all the lies and the betrayals and the stupid games they'd played, and Holly felt a great wave of something darker than simple grief crash over her. She remembered that first week on Santorini, glossy and sunny and perfect. That beautiful week when they'd done nothing but bask in each other and fall madly in love, and she'd believed with every fiber of her being that something so magical, so impossibly vast, could never break or shatter or end. She never could have imagined they'd be standing here now.

Hadn't that been what had driven her all these years? She still couldn't believe it. She'd made it happen herself, but she couldn't believe it had worked.

"None of this matters, anyway," she said. It hurt to swallow. To breathe. "You had the right idea earlier when you walked away. That's what we should do, of course. This never should have been more than a brief, holiday romance years ago. Your whole family was right."

His mouth twisted into something too painful, too dark and cutting, to be a smile.

"Of course," he said, and it hurt all the worse because there was nothing harsh in the way he said it. It sounded like acceptance. Like resignation. "This is the most honest moment I think we've ever had outside a bed, and you think we should end it. I don't know why that surprises me."

"You don't know anything about me," she said, that expression on his face pricking at her, getting deep beneath her skin. "If this night—this marriage—has proved anything, it's that. You are not the authority on *my* honesty. You believed the biggest and worst lie I ever told. And what do I really know about you, anyway? All I knew was that you'd lost your mother when you were young, not how. We might as well be strangers, Theo. Married strangers who are long overdue for a divorce."

He looked at her for what felt like a lifetime, and God, but it hurt. It hurt more than all the rest, or maybe she couldn't tell the difference any longer, and then it hurt even more when he raked his hands through his hair and started moving. For the door, she assumed.

Maybe this really was over, after all. She told herself that should have been a relief.

"I'm not going to chase after you, Holly," he said in a low voice. "You started this four years ago for what I assume are your own good reasons." His expression suggested he assumed nothing of the kind. "You know where I'm staying. If you want to deal with the mess you made, if you think you can bear to stop playing these games, you know where to find me."

"To what end, Theo?" Her own voice was a raw scrape of sound, though it seemed to echo in her like a shout. "To see if we can make all of this that much worse?"

"No. To see if we can make it honest." His mouth crooked and he was too close to her then. Much too close. But she couldn't breathe, anyway. "But I am not optimistic."

"And what do you think that looks like?" she asked. She was whispering now, though the words felt like acid at the back of her throat and she was terribly afraid that the heat on her face was more of the tears she didn't want to let him see. "As far as I can tell we only have two speeds. Wild sex or pure agony. And before you suggest it, I'm not as debauched as you are. I don't quite see myself working out the two extremes with whips and chains in some S and M dungeon somewhere."

"Too bad," he said, his eyes on hers, standing over her with his hands still deep in his pockets and too many shadows on his face. "I think I'd enjoy throwing you over my knee and paddling you until you screamed." Another faint crook of his mouth, this one a kind of dark amusement, and it was like a gift. It gave Holly the smallest bit of hope. "At a bare minimum."

And she reminded herself that what she wanted— what she'd always wanted, however terribly she'd shown it and despite the awful things she'd done to ruin it when she'd had it—was Theo. Not a divorce. It seemed silly to have come all this way, gone through so much, and not make that as clear as possible. No matter how much she really, truly, wanted to run in the opposite direction.

"Or," she suggested, not knowing how she dared when everything was ruined and he was still looking at her as if he might hate her, or maybe it was because of that, "you could kiss me."

He studied her for an eternity, while Holly came face-to-face with the depths of her own cowardice and, conversely, the boundless limits of her capacity to hope. "That doesn't strike me as sufficient punishment."

"That all depends on the kiss, I'd think," she replied.

Theo moved then. He was so big, so beautiful, and that look on his face made her heart cartwheel madly inside her chest. He reached over and took her face between his palms, tipping her face toward his, and it felt new. Perhaps because of the high shoes she wore, perhaps because it had been so very long.

Her heart beat so loud it blocked out the world.

His eyes were so dark they rivaled the night.

Theo bent closer and pressed his lips softly, so softly, against her brow. Then one cheek. Then the other.

And if that careening wildfire that raced through her burned in him, as well, he didn't show it.

"The next time I kiss you—if there is ever a next time—it will be because I trust you, Holly," he told her quietly, almost sweetly, though she understood this was neither of those things. This was a weapon made all the sharper for his restraint, and she felt run clean through. He let go of her then, his dark eyes tearing into her as if he could *see* the way her heart beat, the way it spun and jumped and dipped. "And I don't imagine that's likely to happen anytime soon, do you?"

And Holly couldn't seem to do anything but stand there, ruined all over again, ruined anew, her throat as dry as her stomach was twisted.

He gave her one last look from his too-dark eyes, his mouth so very grim, and then he moved across the hotel room and let himself out into what was left of the night.

CHAPTER SEVEN

THEO WOKE LATE the next morning in what had once been his honeymoon suite to find himself neck-deep in a three-ring circus, which was marginally preferable to the sea of rose petals he'd ordered removed, before he even rolled out of the vast bed.

There were more messages from his office than he could count. His direct employees. Mrs. Papadopoulos, her voice more steely each time. His father. Even his younger brother, Brax, away on a business trip in the far-off reaches of Perth, Australia.

"Your father is trying to reach you, sir," Mrs. Papadopoulos said icily in one of her voice mails. "He has passed by your office. In person. Four times already this morning. To say nothing of the numerous calls from the exceedingly impolite press."

She'd left that message at 9:00 a.m.

"What is it with you and that damned woman?" Brax demanded, sounding as aggrieved as he did far away. "Why must you play these endless games with her to the detriment of the Tsoukatos name? Why can't you call her the mistake she is, divorce her and move on?"

His father was more gruff, and sounded the most furious. As usual.

"I no longer find it amusing to see my successor presented as little more than a pathetic sex machine in the papers," Demetrious Tsoukatos growled. "End this, Theo. Now. *Endaxi*."

Theo tossed his mobile to the side, swung himself out of the bed and onto his feet with a surge of adrenaline and dragged his hands through his hair. Then he forced himself to stop. To breathe. He told himself his pulse was not pounding, that he did not feel that all too familiar wallop of something much too close to betrayal all over again. He told himself that whatever had happened, whatever had spurred all these messages, Holly could not possibly be involved. How could she? He'd left her room not long before dawn, and he'd left *her* in emotional turmoil.

A quick call to the suspiciously overapologetic front desk—never a good sign, Theo thought darkly—brought him a giant carafe of very strong coffee and the papers in question, which Theo spread out before him on the low, solid glass coffee table where once, years before, he'd made a long, sweet feast of his brand-new wife, tasting and savoring every last inch of her delectable body.

It was harder than it should have been to shove those unhelpful images from his head, but Theo managed it.

The screeching, salacious headlines plastered all over the tabloid papers helped him along.

Tsoukatos Savages Scorned Wife! the first hollered, featuring a grainy picture of the two of them in The Chatsfield's lobby, Theo towering over a miserable-looking Holly, appearing to be every inch the savage they claimed he was.

It's been years since shipping tycoon Theo Tsoukatos has been seen in public with the American wife his disapproving father begged him not to take, giving rise to all manner of rumors the notoriously tight-lipped magnate has refused to either confirm or deny... But this emotional scene—captured in the luxurious Barcelona location of the grand Chatsfield Hotel—suggests that an estrangement is the least of the former lovebirds' problems!

Unnamed sources at The Chatsfield dish that while once-infamous Theo checked into the hotel's swanky love nest, a suite created specifically to melt the hardest heart, he's staying there alone!

Can the messy divorce the whole world predicted years ago be far behind?

His jaw ached, and Theo realized he was clenching it. Much too hard. He had to force himself to read the rest of the "article," a series of paragraphs supposedly outlining his and Holly's history while actually making dramatic noises about his wealth and supposed corporate might, before moving on to the other paper.

Reunited at Last? queried the headline. And then just below that: *Or is this just a spot of rearranging deck chairs on the* Titanic?

This one showed a picture of Theo leaving Holly's hotel, The Harrington, with a time stamp in the corner to show it was not exactly at an hour anyone might consider decent, not even in Spain. Inside—on a two-page spread filled with regurgitated photos dating all the way back to their first days on Santorini when Holly had been called his *"unnamed companion"*— he found a picture of him escorting Holly inside, his hand wrapped possessively around her arm, and more breathless speculation.

Are the famously estranged couple finally working out their differences in the high-class embrace of The Harrington, perhaps the most romantic hotel in all of Barcelona? Or is this secret reunion—in the very city where the pair honeymooned following their whirlwind romance and too-hasty wedding almost five years ago—merely a part of a bid for control over the vast Tsoukatos shipping empire?

After all, Holly Tsoukatos stands to be a very wealthy woman in any potential divorce, given fiery tycoon Theo's infamous refusal to sign a prenuptial agreement when they married. A decision a source close to the family claims was widely held to have been "unconscionably stupid."

Brax, Theo assumed, as his father would sooner give himself a frontal lobotomy than speak to the press for any reason, though it could as easily be his secretary.

Representatives for the Tsoukatos family could not be reached for comment, but according to one observer, "It was very flirty and they looked like they were back together. Theo couldn't keep his hands off Holly, and she was clearly loving it."
But is she playing him?

It was only when those last words blurred in front of him that Theo realized he was scowling ferociously. His hands were in hard fists and his temper was kicking in his gut, so loud and so intrusive he was certain he could actually *hear* it. Like a kettle drum.

It took him long moments to realize that it wasn't his temper making the racket in his head—it was someone at his door.

He glared, but the pounding came again. Hard, direct, pointed slaps, like the palm of a hand slamming with significant force into the center of the door.

Theo stalked across the great room and threw it open, welcoming the opportunity to express the depth of his feelings to whatever hapless hotel employee had foolishly happened by into the middle of this mood he was in…

But, of course, it was no hotel employee at all.

It was Holly.

He felt his adrenaline surge again, and then desire with it, that same old unquenchable and ungovernable need that made him act without thinking. Four and a half years ago. Last night. That bone-deep *wanting* that made Theo hate himself. Almost as much as he told himself he hated her then, for doing this to him in the first place. For their entire, twisted and tangled history.

For making him a faithless breaker of vows despite himself, just like his goddamned father.

The moment stretched out, electric and intense.

She was dressed like that chilly version of herself Theo decided he actually detested, in one of those sleek dresses she must have had made for her by the ton, the wild, thick hair he couldn't resist coiled into smooth submission at the nape of her neck. Gone was the creature he'd touched last night, the half-gypsy woman he'd been unable to keep his hands off. He supposed he should thank her for that.

He did not feel anything like *thankful*.

"Why are you here?" Theo demanded, his voice as cool as his temper was hot. "Do you require another photo op? Did the tabloid reporters miss anything?"

"Did you do this?" she threw right back at him. She scowled at him, then brushed past him to enter the suite, her arm barely grazing his bare chest, and Theo was too furious to care the way he should have when everything seemed to simply *light up* inside him at so casual, so tiny, a touch. "Did you sell us out for some labyrinthine reason of your own?"

It was as if she'd switched him on that easily and
no matter how little he might wish it.

She strode inside and despite everything, despite
the whole of their past and even that note of accusation in her voice, Theo allowed himself the pleasure
of watching her move. He'd forgotten the sheer joy of
it, and he told himself he would have to be made of
stone indeed not to notice that sweet roll of her hips,
that smooth, lickable gait she couldn't hide beneath
her elegant clothes. It made him remember her cowboy
boots, her laugh as big as the sky, her hair wrapped
around her like a wild cloak.

It reminded him that the Holly he'd thought he knew
hadn't been a complete figment of his imagination—
she was there, somewhere, beneath all the lies and
the costumes and the hurt. He hadn't made her up out
of thin air.

And then he had the far greater pleasure of watching her come to an abrupt stop as her surroundings
impressed themselves upon her. He heard her breathe
in, sharp and hard, and saw the way she straightened her spine—and he preferred focusing on that
rather than the disquieting things inside of him that
he couldn't seem to shove aside.

He was honest enough to admit, if only to himself,
that he liked that this suite affected her, too. That he
wanted their history to get under her skin as much
as it did his. That even if she was still playing her
damned games, even if the papers were correct and
this was all part of her attempt to start maneuvering
for control of the company, the heat between them

had never been feigned. He remembered, too well, the things that had happened in this suite four and a half years ago. Neither one of them had been faking. At least not that.

"It is so nostalgic, is it not?" he asked acidly, still standing at the door, though he'd closed it behind her. "What a pity I had them clean up all the rose petals you'd so thoughtfully requested. Or I might have asked you to crawl through them, the way you did back then."

Holly turned to look over her shoulder at him, her eyes as blue as the bright Spanish day he could see out the windows beyond her, her wide mouth in a firm line.

"Really?" she asked mildly. As smooth as whatever she'd done to her hair and he liked it as little. "The papers are full of insulting speculation, you almost certainly tipped off the paparazzi yourself or how would they have known to track us to The Harrington, and you want to stand here and talk about a four-and-a-half-year-old bout of oral sex?"

"I think, *agapi mou*, that you may well find it difficult to unearth a single man alive who would not find that particular subject preferable to all others," he observed, a dark kind of amusement coloring his voice as he spoke. "No matter how hard you try to make it sound like some kind of virulent illness we suffered in tandem."

"Yes, Theo," she said in a brittle tone of voice, pivoting around to face him, her sharp heels loud against the marble floor of the arching vestibule, bright sunlight and delicate art all around her, framing her. "I remember. I remember crawling across the floor to you because I couldn't think of a single thing I'd rather do. I remember what happened once I reached you on the couch. I remember what you did with the champagne and I remember how insatiable we both were, that day and the long month after. Are you satisfied? Can we talk about the present?"

"I don't understand," he said, and he refused to acknowledge how difficult it was to maintain that dry, offhanded tone in the wake of all those images she'd thrown at him, all those memories. "Surely you wanted me to stay in this suite so that I would be racked with memories and tortured alive by the past. But now it is the present you'd prefer to discuss? How can I possibly keep up?"

She rolled her eyes and it occurred to Theo that he was as close to enjoying himself as he'd been in... years. That the fury he'd felt rolling through him when he'd read the tabloids, when he'd thrown open the door, had simply gone. Disappeared. It was lost in that stubborn mouth of hers, perhaps, or somewhere on that too-pretty face he still found much too captivating. It had disappeared into the perfect curve of her behind, the sweet indentation of her waist above the intriguing flare of her hips...

Or maybe it was simply that he'd touched her last night, tasted her, and he was an addict. How could he pretend otherwise when he still wanted her—when he always wanted her?

He'd already fallen off the wagon. Why not indulge himself?

As if she could read the rising heat in him, see it right there on his face, Holly moved farther into the room. He followed, studying her as she walked over to the far side of the coffee table and then frowned down at the papers spread out across the glass there.

He'd gotten lost somewhere in his too-vivid memories of Holly on her knees before him, but he remembered the rest of what she'd thrown at him now. Belatedly.

"I did not tip off the paparazzi," he said. She lifted her gaze to his, and he held it as he made his unhurried way around her to settle on the low-slung, soft white sofa. He leaned back, taking his time, watching the way her gaze shifted from his face to the expanse of his chest he hadn't bothered to clothe when he'd gotten out of bed earlier—as if she couldn't help herself, either. "There is little benefit to me in reminding the corporate world that I married a social-climbing American nobody without taking the trouble to protect my family legacy."

"I appreciate you applying such creative license," she said, her tone still so cool that if he hadn't been watching her face so closely, if he hadn't been able to see all that frustrated heat in her blue eyes, he might have believed the ice in it. "But I don't recall any of the articles referring to me as either a social climber or an American nobody."

He inclined his head. "I believe it was inferred."

"Is that why it was so easy for you to believe I'd

cheated on you, Theo?" she asked quietly. He hadn't been expecting it and he told himself that was why it slammed into him like that. "Because that was what you thought of me? Because deep down, or maybe not so deep at all, you imagined cheating on you with some random tourist was exactly what a social-climbing American nobody would do?"

Theo fought back the urge to defend himself—again. Or to offer her any explanations for the things he'd done after she'd torn him apart. He owed her neither, he assured himself. Instead, he lounged back against the sofa and spread his arms along the length of it, keeping his eyes trained on her face as he did, watching all the reactions she fought to hide.

Pretending he didn't feel each and every one of them in the hungry length of his sex, as if it was her mouth instead.

"Why did you come here?" he asked after a moment. He could see a faint flush high on her cheekbones, and he ordered himself not to react to it. Not to give in to the urges of flesh, of memory. Not yet. "Surely a telephone call would have sufficed. Why come in person, thereby throwing fuel on the fire, if the blaze wasn't of your own making?"

"I suppose I wanted to watch you lie to me in person," she replied, and he suspected she knew it stung. He forced himself to shrug it off.

"And why are you back in all that armor you wear?" he asked instead of responding to her dig. Instead of surging to his feet and hauling her against him, then rolling her beneath him at last. Instead of handling her with his body, with the passion that had always been there between them, a connection nothing ever seemed to break or diminish. *A compulsion*, he thought. *A damned addiction, nothing more.* "What do you imagine I might do to you, that you should require it?"

She stood taller, if that was possible. More rigid. "Armor? Where I come from we call this a dress."

"Last night you came to find me in the clubs dressed like the girl I remember," Theo said, as if he was speaking words of love. Or sex. As if there was a difference where the two of them were concerned. As if the poetry between them had ever been anything but dark. "Was that only for the dark of night? Or was it yet another manipulation? Another role for you to play as you tried your best to bend me to your will?"

"It was an outfit appropriate for the circumstances," Holly said, her voice as sharp as glass. "Not a grand conspiracy. I'm sorry to disappoint you."

"And what circumstances are these, then, that require you dress as an imposter of yourself?" he asked. He let his eyes move over her. "You must realize that I have always found Holly Holt, the charmingly innocent adventuress who happened upon me on a sunny Greek island one summer, far more attractive than Holly Tsoukatos, the brittle and scheming society wife who drains my bank accounts and my patience in equal measure."

"I'll be certain to let you know the next time I require your input on how I dress." A flash of temper in those blue eyes. A cold curve to her lips. "Let me offer you a hint. It won't be soon."

"Yet you raced here to speak to me. Dressed like this again when only last night you showed me the Holly I remember for the first time in years. How can I imagine it is anything but deliberate?" He made a show of leaning back, of relaxing. He even smiled, though he could feel the sharp edge to it—and more, could see it reflected in the way she pulled in a breath. "Last night's Holly was the carrot, I suppose. This must be the stick."

She sniffed, and eyed him. "Should I have dressed like you, Theo? Then made my way through the city half-naked and rumpled with sleep? What grand theories would you have come up with then?"

"What do you want?" he asked again, softly. "And why did you feel you had to put on your favorite disguise to come here and ask for it?"

Holly looked something like shaken for a moment, but then she blinked, and he was almost convinced he'd imagined it. Almost.

"I think we should concentrate on the fact we're all over the papers again," she said tightly—as if this was hard for her, Theo thought, and God help him, but he *wanted* this to be hard for her. He wanted all of this to be hard for her.

Because if it was hard, it must matter. *It must.*

He refused to think about why he found that so critical.

"I don't think so," he said.

"You don't think we should worry about the fact

the tabloids are stalking us?" She sounded incredulous, and irritated besides. "Telling melodramatic stories about us all over again?"

"I don't think that's why you're here. I don't think that's why you went to such care with your appearance, the better to look cool and polished when you arrived." He let his gaze linger on her, let her see what she'd made him, steel and stone. "I don't think the tabloids are anything but an excuse."

"For what?" She lifted her chin and her blue eyes were chilly, but her voice betrayed her. It was too soft. It hinted at too much turmoil beneath.

"For this." He didn't move any closer to her then. He didn't stand up and put his hands on her—he didn't have to. It was as if they were gripped in the same tight fist, held close and trapped. He could feel the constriction of it. He could see the way it made her breathing shallow. He could feel it inside of him, heat and longing, and something far darker besides. "I'd be surprised if you slept at all last night. You wanted to race here as soon as possible this morning to take the measure of my guilt."

She only stared back at him. Her blue eyes were bright, perhaps too bright. He could see the pulse in her throat, beating too fast. Giving her away no matter how she tried to hide in her elegant costume and haughty demeanor. He could see. He knew.

"You seem crippled with shame," she pointed out drily.

The lie came easily. "I feel no shame, Holly. No guilt. All of that is yours to bear."

"Yes," she said in a whisper. "Two wrongs are largely renowned, I've found, for making a right. Everybody always says so."

"There was one wrong," he told her, very deliberately, very clearly. "One lie. And everything that followed came directly from that. Will we argue this forever? Is this why you came here this morning? To see if my answer would magically change?"

"I didn't think your answer would magically change," Holly said quietly, and the way she looked at him then made something in him very nearly shudder. He told himself it didn't matter, just as he'd been telling himself *she* didn't—and yet here they were. "But I persist in imagining you might."

He'd changed. He'd been leveled. But he only stared back at her and refused to admit that. Not now. Not here.

"It didn't matter who those other women were," he said then, and he did nothing to ease the blow. He did nothing to make it better—if anything, he let the bitter truth of it spill out where it would. "All I ever saw was you."

Holly stopped lying to herself in a sudden rush as Theo's harsh sucker punch connected, a direct hit, then reverberated through her as if he'd delivered a street fighter's kick to the back.

Hard enough to maim, she thought dimly, if she let it.

"Oddly," she heard herself say, as if from some great distance, from somewhere her ears weren't ringing and she felt less dizzy with reaction and regret alike, "that doesn't help at all."

Theo was lounging back against the all-white sofa, looking dark and dangerous and something far more compelling than simply delicious as he sat there, all of that hard heat in his dark eyes and the vast, sculpted expanse of his naked chest beneath.

Would this be easier if he was less beautiful? Holly wondered.

When he'd answered his door wearing nothing but dark athletic trousers low on his hips and a scowl, she'd nearly toppled over. This was the Theo she remembered, this impossibly beautiful creature, all sinew and strength, even when it looked as if he'd done nothing more today than roll out of his bed. He exuded sex. Danger. He was male and hot and astonishingly magnetic, and more than that, he was imprinted deep in her soul. Every place he'd touched her last night thrilled to the sight of him and then ached, long and low. Like a fire she'd never put out.

She stopped pretending she could. Or that she'd ever wanted to, because she hadn't. Not really.

"What part of me?" she asked instead, before she knew she meant to speak—and maybe it was better that way. There was less chance she'd edit herself. Less opportunity to hide in plain sight. "What part did you see?"

Theo blinked, and then went still—so still that Holly had to replay what she'd just said to make sure she'd really said it out loud.

Oh, yes. She really, truly had.

It was like another kick, and this time, she was the one who'd delivered it. Shock waves rolled through her, and she could see them in him, too, though he didn't move.

No particular shame in telling a lie, I suppose, her father had told her once a long time ago, when she'd been a young girl dealing with the usual trials of middle school and the duplicity of some of her peers. *A person has reasons. The shame is in holding on to the lie when the truth is right in front of you. The shame is in pretending the lie* is *the truth. A lie might not kill you, darlin', but shame always will.*

"I beg your pardon?" Theo asked with an exaggerated politeness that almost made Holly laugh. But she didn't. This was much too important.

"Which part of me did you see while you were drowning your troubles in other women?" she asked instead, as distinctly and directly as she could.

She didn't understand what was happening to her, what she was feeling. The idea of him with other women made her feel sick, as she imagined he meant it to—but then, the logical part of her brain knew he was right. She was the one who had brought infidelity into their marriage, whether real or imagined. She'd opened that door. She was the one who'd broken the trust between them, who'd claimed she'd broken the vows they'd made to each other. How could she hold him to a standard she'd insisted he believe she'd ignored herself? When she'd left him to marinate in what remained after her tortured "confession"?

But it was more insidious than that, Holly knew.

It was far sicker, if she let herself consider it fully. It was all right there in what he'd said. That he'd *seen* her, even when she was far away. That it was all *about* her, somehow.

She didn't understand why that felt like a gift. Like something almost romantic, in a deeply twisted way, given their circumstances. Only that it did. And that no matter how messed up it all was, she would accept it.

And she didn't care what that made her.

"I don't know what game this is," he growled at her.

"My hands?" Holly asked, ignoring him. She moved toward him, letting the stilettos she wore accentuate the sway of her hips, noting the way his dark eyes dropped hungrily and stayed there. Watching her. Enjoying her. "My hair?"

"Not scraped back and hidden like that, no," he muttered, almost as if he couldn't help himself, and Holly felt that everywhere. It ignited deep inside her, rolling outward, dark smoke and thick flames, making her feel molten and undone.

And powerful, somehow. As if he really was still hers, after all. After everything.

She stopped moving when she stood before him at last, just slightly inside his sprawled-out legs. He didn't sit up straighter or do anything to suggest he was reacting to her nearness—but she could see that hunger in his eyes, so dark, so damned hot, and it was enough.

It made that fire in her arc higher. It consumed everything.

It was all that mattered.

CHAPTER EIGHT

HOLLY REACHED UP behind her, taking her time, arching her back as she did it so her breasts pressed against the bodice of her dress, and plucked the pins from her hair. One after the next. Lazily, with her gaze on his. Her hair uncoiled slowly and then, when she pulled out the last pin, fell in a thick line to her shoulders.

That was when she shook it out, using her whole body, running her fingers through the mass of it, letting the blond waves swirl and then fall where they liked. While Theo sat there below her, gazing up at her as if he was having a religious experience, his arms spread wide while his hands gripped the back of the couch, his knuckles as white as the fabric beneath him.

"Where else did you see me?" she asked him, and she could hear the roughness in her voice. Sex and longing, the long ache of lost years, the bittersweet need still so ripe after so many betrayals. It only spurred her on. "Which part of me drew you in the most?"

"You shouldn't have left me, Holly."

He didn't mean to say that. She could see that truth as plainly as if he'd confessed it, could see the torment in his dark gaze and the way his hands dug into the sofa, and later, perhaps, she would tell herself that that was why she sank down on her knees then, placing herself squarely between his outstretched legs.

Much as she had years before.

His dark gaze ignited, then went molten.

Holly found she was biting her lip.

She didn't think. She didn't worry any longer. She let go of the great hoard of pain and hurt feelings and betrayal and horror at what had happened between them. What she'd done. What he'd done. She ignored all of that and reached out instead, sliding her palms onto his knees.

He went taut beneath her. She could see the tightness of the smooth muscles of his hard chest before her as well as she could feel them beneath her hands, and she reveled in the sensation. In the pure, sweet glory that was touching him again.

Theo. His name was like a light inside of her, so bright it hurt.

She could feel the heat of his skin through his trousers, and she wanted nothing more than to tip forward and taste that tempting shallow between his pectoral muscles, where she knew he tasted of salt and musk, all man, and in a moment like this, all hers.

Holly knelt forward, running her palms up over his knees and onto the shelf of his thighs, feeling something bloom within her at his checked breath, at the jagged way he expelled it. Higher she moved. Then higher still.

"What are you doing?"

She smiled slightly. "You can't guess? It really has been a long time."

"Tell me what this is, Holly. Now." An order, almost barked out—but the hard lines of his face spoke only of need, of want. Of barely restrained passion, and Holly smiled wider. "Tell me what you want."

"There can only be a few options, I think," she murmured, gauging his response as she traced the heavy muscles of his strong thighs, testing their mouthwatering strength and density, letting the spark of it, the sheer tactile excitement, run all over her. Through her. Touching him was almost as good as letting him touch her. In some ways it was better. "Why don't you pick one?"

"Holly…" But her name trailed off into a muttered Greek curse when she reached the tops of his thighs and, without pausing, covered the straining heat of him with one hand.

God, but she wanted him. She had always wanted him—perhaps she always would. From the moment she'd glanced up from her table in that long-ago café, she'd been struck with this same electrical charge of pure need. No matter what had happened since. No matter what might happen next. He burned so hot, even through the trousers he wore, that it took her a moment to realize that she was breathing as heavily as he was as she reached beneath his waistband and pulled him out.

He was so proud, so male. He was perfect.

And it took a very long time to register the fact that he'd said her name again, and then, when she did, to drag her gaze back up to his.

His was a dark storm, elemental and demanding, and she felt gooseflesh rise all over her, sweeping from the back of her neck down her arms, rippling over her to make her nipples into hard, needy pebbles while between her legs there was nothing but wet heat and yearning.

Nothing mattered but this. Nothing mattered but him.

She wrapped her fingers around his length, marveling in the softness of his skin with all that steel beneath, and he cursed again. Harsher this time.

"I told you last night." But his voice was made of sand and greed, gritty and needy at once, and all she could see in those dark eyes of his was this. Sex. *Yes.* Now. "I don't trust you."

"Then by all means, Theo," Holly murmured, trusting the hardest part of him in her hand, trusting the faintest of shudders she could feel in his powerful body beneath her, trusting that this was the right thing with every part of her that shivered and ached and *demanded*, "don't sully yourself. Don't kiss me if you don't want to. I don't care."

And then she bent her head and took him deep into her mouth.

He almost lost it, like the untrained boy he hadn't been in more years than he could count.

Her mouth was wicked and hot, moving over him as if she wanted to learn him all over again. With her sweet tongue, the faint scrape of her teeth.

She took him deep, wrapping her hand around the base of him and humming her approval, and Theo tipped his head back and let himself pretend.

That this was a simple exercise, need and heat. That she wanted him without any ulterior motives. Without any agenda.

With her between his legs, her mouth like a sacrament and a filthy little curse at once, he could almost believe it.

Or in any case, he didn't care. He wanted this to go on forever.

As if she agreed, she set a lazy little rhythm, alternating between the deep embrace of her clever mouth and the teasing of her lips, her tongue, against the tip of his need. And Theo stopped caring about the rest of it. Her lies, her abandonment. The whole of their tortured whirlwind of a marriage.

He dug his fingers deep into the fragrant softness of her hair and he let her take him as she liked, however she liked.

But when he neared the edge, he pulled her back, opening his eyes to look down at her. He knew that expression. It made his chest tight, made that fire in him roar. Her flushed cheeks, her glassy blue eyes. The way she shivered and swayed, moving restlessly, as if her own need was on the verge of sweeping her away, though she was the one giving pleasure rather than receiving it.

"I missed you," he gritted, and thought he'd regret that later, but he couldn't seem to care about that the way he knew he should. He rubbed his hand over the heated silk of her cheek. "I missed this. But no. Not like this. Not…"

"Please, Theo." Her voice was husky. Needy. If she was playing a game, he thought, she'd gotten as caught up in it as he was. "I want to. I want *you*."

How could he refuse when she sucked him deep again, making soft, greedy noises that shot straight into him like lightning? How could he refuse her anything at all?

And this time, when he hit that edge, he let himself fall right over it, shouting out her name.

When Theo could think again, she was sitting back on her heels with those sexy shoes still on her feet, looking up at him, a deeply satisfied expression on her face. He studied her for a moment while his heart did its best to claw its way out of his chest. She looked glossy and replete, and he couldn't remember ever wanting her more.

And the time for thinking, clearly, was over.

So he reached down and hauled her to him, smiling to himself at the desperate little sound she made as she came. It didn't take much to put her where he wanted her, beneath him on that long white sofa, where he could stretch out above her, then reach down between them to tug the smooth column of her dress to her hips, exposing her femininity to his gaze, his hands, his wishes.

He wanted to kiss her more than he wanted his next mouthful of air. He wanted the crush of her lips, her perfect taste against his tongue, her mouth beneath his. But he refused to indulge himself no matter the temptation. No matter that she tilted her head back, as if she was daring him.

"You have to earn that," he told her.

He expected her to say something then, to tease him or try to lighten the moment, or perhaps to push him off her altogether as he half expected she'd do, but she only watched him, her breath slightly stuttered and her blue eyes so bright they gleamed.

Heat. Need. And what temper there was only making the fire of it burn higher.

Theo shifted down, pressing a kiss to the slope of her belly above the lacy edge of her panties. He shouldered his way into position, drawing one long, perfectly formed leg up and over the back of the sofa and letting the other fall to the floor. He held her soft, shapely thighs apart and then he moved in closer, inhaling her scent, warm and female and aroused.

He glanced up to find her watching him, the color high in her cheeks and her lips slightly parted, her hair wild around her like some kind of sensual halo, and he thought he'd never seen anything more beautiful in his life.

Then he simply bent his head, pressed his mouth over the damp center of her need, panties and all, and sucked her in. Hard.

Holly went rigid around him and then broke apart, that easily.

She heard herself cry out as she flew over the side

of the earth, but then she was lost in the shaking, the glorious shuddering, the sweet magic that was Theo.

Only and ever Theo.

And when she came back to that couch with a jolt, Theo had shifted to peel her panties down her legs, then toss them aside with her shoes before settling himself back between her thighs.

"Theo," she said, but laughed, because her voice was a stranger's, and he ignored her, anyway, holding her in place with one hard, strong hand against her belly and the other wrapped around her hip.

His gaze met hers like lightning. Like whole storms. His hard mouth curved in obvious male satisfaction, and that alone sent a wild charge spinning through her, making that fire leap inside of her anew.

And then he bent down and licked his way into her with no barrier at all this time, and Holly forgot about anything else.

He tasted her as if she was precious, as if he was ravenous. He took her with his talented mouth, making her arch and writhe and fall apart beneath him. He drove her up into all of that gleaming wildness again, using his teeth and his tongue, the pressure of his mouth and the sweet reach of his fingers, again and again, until she was bucking and sobbing.

His name. As if it was a prayer.

Until she would have promised him anything and given him more, and might have, for all she knew.

Only then did he throw her over that edge again, holding her as she shook, and then sucking the center of her need deep into his mouth just as she started to come down, which cast her off all over again.

She was wild when she was herself again, all of that fire and bright passion slamming through her veins, pooling inside of her, making her reach out for him—but he was already there.

He was speaking in Greek, murmuring dark words like incantations all around them as he sat back, pulling her with him. She climbed over him, straddling him when he urged her into position, feeling desperate as he settled them both back against the couch and then held her hips where he wanted them. Where she wanted them, too.

Holly could feel him, hard and hot and *right there*, teasing the heart of her with the hard edge of his need, making her shudder and yearn.

"Theo," she whispered. *"Please."*

And he thrust into her, deep and sure, bringing them both home that easily.

They both gasped at the sleek fit, the sweet heat that was as perfect as it had always been, and their eyes caught. Held. And then Theo gripped her hips in his talented hands as he started to move her against him.

Up and then down. *Slow.* So slow. Teasing them both.

Killing them both.

Killing *her.*

"Hurry," she ordered him, almost crossly, and he only laughed up at her.

And then he took his own sweet time.

He built that fire inside her high, much higher than before, so high Holly thought it might kill them both before he was done. Because surely no one could survive this. Surely *she* couldn't survive this. Theo's hands dug into her bottom as he controlled the pace, the depth, the rhythm, and she didn't bother to fight him. Instead, Holly surrendered.

To his masterful touch, to the fire he made dance inside her as he pleased, to that look of sheer wonder in his dark gaze. To him, the way she always had, and her reward was the glorious thing he wove around them with each deep, delicious thrust.

And this time, she came apart as she rode him, writhing there above him. Her head fell back and he held her even tighter as she arched into him, pounding out his own release into her as if they had always been joined like this. As if they'd never been apart.

As if this was the only thing that mattered.

As if nothing else ever could.

And she stayed there, wrapped in his arms, for what felt like a very long time. So long that she almost let herself believe that she could stay there forever...

But as much as Holly tried to hold on to all of that magic, reality intruded. Theo shifted beneath her and she climbed off him, her dress still crumpled up around her hips. She stood on shaky legs as she smoothed it back into place, and did her best to look at anything but him when he stood there next to her and tucked himself back into his trousers. He nudged her cast-off shoes toward her with one foot and it seemed like the hardest thing in all the world to step into them again.

"Theo…" she began, and she had no idea what she was going to say. She had no idea how to fix what she'd broken or even how to explain it in any way he'd understand when she could hardly understand it herself. She had no idea what she'd do if he shifted what had happened here into something cruel, no matter how much she might have deserved it.

"Are you hungry?" he asked, and there was something gruff in his voice, something she couldn't read in the too-dark gaze he trained on her then, as if he was as loath to let go of this moment as she was. She found she wanted to believe that far more than was wise. Much less safe. But she couldn't seem to help herself around this man. Hadn't that always been the case? "I find I am ravenous."

"I…I don't…"

Holly didn't know what she wanted to say. What she *could* say, for that matter. There were storms inside of her, threatening her foundations and rattling her walls, but she didn't know how she could possibly explain any of that to him. How she could look at him, even now, and love him so much despite the fact he still terrified her on some deep, fundamental level. How could she explain it to him when she could hardly explain it to herself?

And Theo only watched her, his dark gaze locked to hers, as if he could do it forever. As if he already knew all those things that scrapped and tumbled inside of her. As if he could read every single thing that moved in the depths of her, when she knew he couldn't—when even she couldn't.

"Yes," she whispered, surrender and something else twisting around and around inside of her, making her feel very nearly giddy, "I'm very hungry, in fact."

And when he smiled at her then, it felt like the sun rising after a very long, very dark, very dangerous night. Like a victory far greater and far more critical than a simple meal.

Like hope.

It was a perfect day.

Later, Holly would remember it as if each part had been spread out before her in a series of postcards, capturing each moment as it happened. A leisurely meal to start, filled with all manner of local delicacies. Then the lazy stroll along Las Ramblas, winding their way through the city, side by side. Wandering in and out of the narrow streets and sudden squares that made up the Gothic Quarter. And talking all the while, as if they liked each other the way they once had. About the world. About Theo's job and his aspirations and what it was like to fill his father's mighty shoes. About Holly's charity work, and the parts of it she enjoyed.

As if they had no past. As if they were on a date and could curate the stories of their lives to best suit the moment, to best amuse the other. As if there was nothing between them but a cloudless blue day in a beautiful city, and the whole of a great, bright future ahead.

As night fell, they stood together on a rooftop terrace with the sparkle of the Port of Barcelona spread out before them, with views that swept over the Barceloneta Quarter and beyond—but Holly was only dimly aware of the scope of it beyond its shine. It was as if she was no longer capable of seeing anything but Theo. As if he blocked out the whole of the world.

He always has, a little voice inside her reminded her. Warned her. *Don't you remember? You spent six months in his shadow. Six months and you forgot who you were...*

"Are you cold?" Theo's voice was warm and close, and Holly shoved that little voice aside, focusing on him instead. His mouth curved as his gaze traced its way over her face. "You shivered."

This was what she wanted, she told herself staunchly, flipping through the postcard-perfect day in her mind as she tipped her head back to meet that dark gaze of his. She'd suffered for four years without him and she'd still come back. This was where she ought to be, right here within Theo's reach.

This is where you belong.

Holly told herself that had to be true, because nothing else made sense.

Because despite all appearances to the contrary and her own behavior four years ago, she wasn't her mother. She hadn't taken off with another man, no matter what she might have let her husband believe at the time. And she'd come back, hadn't she? She wasn't anything like her mother.

She couldn't be like her mother. She refused.

"If you keep frowning at me," Theo pointed out in that deceptively mild way of his that made every hair on her body prickle into awareness, "I'll be forced to conclude that our little bubble of peace has imploded. And I don't know about you, Holly, but I am not quite ready to face the things that need facing on the other side of this."

"That sounds ominous." She had to force the words out, force them to sound light. Airy. A part of the night around them, the music and the laughter that soared up from the rooftop where they stood toward the stars that were only then starting to show themselves high above.

"Not at all," Theo said. "Merely realistic."

He reached over and took her hand, playing idly with the rings he'd put there, the way he always had. As if he was reclaiming her, or her hand—or simply reminding himself, perhaps. She wasn't sure she wanted to know. When he looked up at her again, there was a certain resolve in his dark gaze, a particular set to his mouth.

And Holly wasn't ready.

She didn't want *realism*. She didn't want answers. There were no shadows tonight, no disappearances. They were here, together. He was warm and real, and she still wanted him so badly it made her quiver inside, and that, she thought, should be the only thing that mattered. It should be the only thing she let sway her, one way or the other.

"I want to dance," she told him, before he could speak. "This is Barcelona, is it not?"

His dark eyes gleamed in the gathering dark. "It is."

"Then I want to dance until dawn and then I want to roll around in a bed with you, naked and wild like it's our own kind of dancing, and I might want to do it all over again tomorrow. And then again." Holly slid her arms up around his neck and she held on when he went still, letting her body graze his, letting that sweet electricity burn hot between them the way it always did. She held on because she thought that if she didn't, she might fall off the side of the world entirely, and this time she doubted she'd come back. "What about that for reality?"

Theo's hands came to her hips and held her there, gently enough. His dark, dark gaze saw much too deep. Holly found she was holding her breath, waiting for him to render judgment in that ruthless way of his, but then, impossibly, that hard mouth of his curved.

It felt like a reprieve. Like a bone-deep relief.

"As you wish, *agapi mou*," he said, quiet and rich. "You have two days."

And though his voice was low and dark, it was the first time he'd said those words without the sarcastic, mocking edge she'd come to expect.

My love.

Almost as if he meant them. As if this was real, after all. Holly shivered again. Harder, and it made her breasts scrape against his chest. It made her knees feel watery. It made her burn for him, hot and needy and wild. It made her want all kinds of things she was afraid to admit she wanted.

But Theo only smiled, as if he knew that, too.

CHAPTER NINE

Is this a second honeymoon for Theo and Holly?
Or a calculated attempt at a honey trap in the
city where it all started?

HOLLY SIGHED AT the sight of yet another tabloid headline screaming at her from a newsagent's tucked into an alcove in the busy Gothic Quarter.

It had been two more days, as Theo had promised. Two perfect days in beautiful Barcelona, and she and Theo had spent most of that time lost entirely in each other. Wandering the romantic streets, partaking of the marvelous food. Dancing in the clubs as Holly had requested, then exploring each other later, until it all blurred together into a potent mix of sex and touch, rhythm and music, the sea and the sun. The architectural magic of Gaudí that made the city into something out of a dream, the look on Theo's dark face when he moved inside of her and drove them both insane...

She wrenched her attention away from the shrieking paper and was glad she was wearing sunglasses large enough to disguise her face to some degree—though there was no disguising Theo. He turned heads wherever he went, cutting a swath through the crowds as tourists and locals alike tripped over themselves to get out of his way, and then to gawk at him as he passed. He had that much obvious power stamped deep into every inch of his athletic body. That much offhanded intensity.

"I don't understand the tabloid fascination," Holly said in an undertone, pressing closer to his side as they navigated around a group of British girls taking jubilant self-portraits down an ancient street with the Barcelona Cathedral rising up in the background. "Surely there's a surly pop star behaving badly somewhere. Thousands of minor celebrities clamoring for attention. Why does anyone care what we do?"

Theo had spent the better part of their rare breakfast outside of the bedroom firing off emails and messages from his mobile, and had only concluded a phone call—conducted in low, emphatic Greek that had not sounded at all friendly—moments before. He slid her a look then that reminded Holly of the way he'd woken her up earlier in her wide, soft bed at The Harrington, sliding deep inside of her from behind and bringing her halfway to bliss before she'd completely woken up to find herself, quite literally, in his hands.

He smiled when she flushed hot at the memory, and she was struck—not for the first time—with the sense of losing her place, somehow. As if, should she only allow herself, she could tip over into that dark gaze of his, tumble deep into him and never surface again. It had always been like that. And some part of her had never wanted anything else.

Some part of her still didn't, no matter how much that frightened her at the same time, down deep into her bones.

"I doubt anyone particularly cares about us in specific," he said after a moment as they turned a tight corner and started down another old and echoing street, packed with pedestrians as the morning inched toward another stunningly blue midday. "Not really. I suspect it has a great deal more to do with where we're staying."

Holly blinked at that. "Why would anyone care where we're staying?"

Theo's mobile buzzed in his hand. He glanced at it, but then returned his attention to Holly, considering her for a moment as he slipped it back into his pocket. Or perhaps it was his own words he was considering, she thought, as he appeared to choose them much more carefully these days.

"Do you not know?" he asked in that cool way of his that made her think of the boardrooms they claimed he dominated merely by entering, just as his legendary father always had done. Chrome and glass towers, powerful men and Theo in the middle of everything, ruling over it with this new iron will of his he wore so easily and wielded so matter-of-factly. If possible, she found this incarnation of his even more compelling than the Theo she'd thought she'd known before, though she hardly dared admit it. "I assumed that was why you chose to stay at The Harrington in the first place. To pick a side in their fight with The Chatsfield, in this as in everything else."

Holly didn't realize she'd stopped walking until he took her arm, drawing her out of the flow of foot traffic into the mouth of a winding little alley, tucked between two medieval buildings in the maze of the old city. She didn't know why she felt almost breathless, as if she'd been running, or climbing up a steep hill.

As if he'd accused her of something significantly more terrible than her choice of accommodations.

"I can confidently assure you, Theo, that if a couple of hotel chains are having pitched battles in the streets—if it's *West Side Story* but with a lot of concierges and bellhops—" she held his gaze as she continued "—as delightful as that sounds, I am blissfully unaware of it."

It was only when Theo studied her face for a long moment rather than replying that she recognized her tone was, perhaps, a shade or two too strident. She thought he might call her on that but he didn't, though she felt the heat of his stare deep inside of her, kicking up brushfires she wasn't sure she cared to examine too closely.

"The Chatsfields are trying to take over the Harrington Hotels," he said. He propped a shoulder against the far wall of the narrow alleyway, he never shifted his gaze from hers and she felt she needed to dig her fingers into the wall behind her to keep from plummeting so far into him she'd never come out again. "I believe an initial offer was somewhat unexpectedly refused. Feelings of betrayal, an enduring struggle between two forces, complicated negotiations." He shrugged, with his mouth as well as his shoulder, in that deeply Mediterranean way of his that, despite herself, she found fascinating. "I suppose our troubled marriage must seem like an excellent metaphor."

"For a set of boring corporate shenanigans?" Her voice was dry, and she ignored how she felt about his use of the word *troubled*, how it echoed around inside of her and then sank hard, like a stone. "Yes. Very metaphoric indeed."

His gaze seemed to sharpen then, and something changed in the air between them, so dramatic she thought for an instant it was the weather. A sudden summer storm, perhaps, swept in from the sea. But the blue sky above remained bright and perfect, and only Theo's dark gaze altered at all.

"These are family businesses, Holly," he said, and though his tone was mild, that look in his eyes was anything but, and she wished she couldn't *feel* that the way she did then. As if it was reproof and challenge at once. As if it hummed through her, making everything inside of her shudder precariously in its wake. "Everyone involved tends to take what happens with them quite seriously. And very personally."

She could have told him she knew all about pointless family businesses, such as they were, and the heartbreaking struggle to maintain them in the face of one impossible obstacle and staggering setback after the next. She could have mentioned that it was all an exercise in futility, in the end. That the entity with the most money always, always won. In the case of her father's ranch, that had been the bank, no matter how hard Holly had worked to raise money to help pay off the mortgage. In the case of her marriage, it would always be Theo, as her battered heart attested every time she looked at him. Why should a set of luxury hotels escape the same sad fate?

But she suspected Theo didn't want to hear all that.

"Then I imagine the family members involved would make a far better focus for intrusive tabloid articles, wouldn't they?" she asked him instead.

Except she wasn't really asking. And there was no pretending that wasn't an aggressive tone of voice, completely inappropriate for a quiet conversation about things that shouldn't matter to her in the least, like the Chatsfield and Harrington hotel dynasties. She tilted her chin up, and that, too, was belligerent. She felt it, but she couldn't seem to help herself. And Holly thought they would topple over the cliff of this strange tension straight into one of the flash fights they'd used to have so often four years ago, and some part of her yearned for it, because they'd always ended the same way, all of that fury and temper and volume rolling right over into the nearest bed...

But instead, Theo reached across the alley and picked up a strand of the hair she'd left down this morning because she knew he liked it better that way, wrapping the blond wave around and around his finger.

For a moment, that was the whole world.

They both stared at his hand, and the spiral of her hair he wound tighter and tighter around his index finger. Outside their shadowed, surprisingly private alley, the old city bustled and swirled, its insistent energy making its own kind of music and swelling around them. Up above, the Spanish sky beamed. And here in their tiny little circle, Holly's heart beat so loud and so hard she was certain it drowned out all the rest. Maybe the entire planet.

"What is it that distresses you so much about the tabloid attention?" Theo asked after a moment—or perhaps a decade—inched by. But she couldn't seem to find her voice, and he kept on. "Is it that you worry the focus on our relationship will force you into finally making a decision about this marriage? Or that it may well compel me to do so for the both of us?"

It was panic that rocketed through her then, making her pulse a wild scream, her chest so tight it hurt.

"If our marriage survives or fails based on the fantasies of tabloid writers, then we deserve whatever we get," Holly whispered fiercely, and she tried to shove the panic back down into a box inside her, to hide it away, to pretend it was something else.

Sex. Fury. *Something.*

He tugged gently enough on that strand of her hair, and she felt it like an electric current, making everything inside of her clench tight. As if all she'd ever been, or would become, was stranded here in this tight little space with him, waiting for whatever came next.

Waiting for him to make the decision so you don't have to? a little voice asked, sounding as snide as those tabloid articles did, as judgmental and arch, and as damaging. *Is that what you're hoping will happen here?*

"Or is it that you don't like all this speculation about your motives?" Theo asked quietly, his words like stones, dropping through her one after the next. "After all, they only claim I am a fool for a pretty face. They suspect you of a far darker agenda. Does it hit a bit too close to home?"

And Holly couldn't help the misery that flooded her then. It came on so fast and so hard she understood it had never been far away at all—it had only been waiting. It washed over her, swamping her, and she couldn't hide any of it. He was right there, watching as it moved through her, with those dark, clever eyes of his that had always seen far too much, anyway.

It was as if he was inside of her, as if there was nothing that could keep him out, and Holly still didn't know if she craved that connection or feared it. She still didn't know what she wanted. Only that she couldn't seem to live without this man, no matter how torn she felt when he was near.

"You don't understand," she said unsteadily now, casting around for some kind of explanation when she feared there was none. None that made sense, not even in her own mind. "My father loved my mother *so much*. He was crazy about her. She was everything to him. She left him when I was a little girl and our entire lives were arranged around it. Not the fact of her absence, but his bedrock certainty that she would return. She never did." She pulled in a ragged breath. "And still, when he died, right there at the end, he called out her name."

Theo didn't say a word, he only watched, steady and unyielding, and Holly didn't question why that made her feel more balanced. Why he made her feel strong when she was deeply afraid he was her greatest weakness. But whatever it was, that dark patience of his made her capable of taking another deep breath, and then continuing.

"When I met you, I fell so hard I think I had bruises for months afterward. Maybe years." She shook her head. "I didn't know anything. I was all alone in the world, and then there was you, and over the six months we were together I got lost in that. Completely lost. I was terrified that I'd end up just like my father."

"Surely that would only be cause for concern had I left you," Theo said, and on some level, Holly understood that only a couple of days ago, he would have said that with a harsh edge, calculated to draw blood. That it would have sliced her in half and he would have reveled in the cutting.

Today his voice was soft. Quiet.

She swallowed. "People leave each other all the time, Theo."

"So this was, what? A proactive attempt to forestall pain by inflicting it yourself? Before I could make your history repeat itself, somehow?"

It would have been different if he'd sounded angry. Even hurt. But he only sounded curious, and that was why she could keep going.

"I don't know," she whispered. "All I knew was that I had to get away from you before there wasn't any of me left."

His gaze kindled into a kind of blaze, but he didn't move. His expression remained calm, and she wondered what that cost him. And deep inside of her, Holly felt something crack wide-open.

"Theo," she whispered, unable to stop herself. Unable to think better of what she was doing. "I'm so sorry. I hope you know that."

He slid his hands up to hold her cheeks between them, and she'd never seen the look he wore then. It was a naked thing, as if she wasn't the only one breaking open—an idea she couldn't quite accept.

"I am, too," he said in a very low, very gruff voice that seemed to wind its way deep into her bones.

"That I left you?"

"That, yes." Something that looked like pain moved across his face, and it echoed within her, making her feel warped. Altered. "And that I chose to respond to it in such a childish, tit-for-tat way. Who did that serve? Just because I thought you'd broken your vows, that didn't mean I should have, too."

"Theo…"

But that fierce light in his gaze stopped her.

"I meant it when I said forever, Holly," he whispered harshly. "I hope you believe me. I really did."

And then he bent his head and finally—*finally*—fit his mouth to hers.

He kissed her as if he'd never stopped loving her. He kissed her as if the taste of her was precious. He angled his jaw to take the kiss deeper, he held her face in his hands and he kissed her as if it was a new vow. As if it was an apology and a prayer at once.

A new start. As if the past didn't matter at all, and couldn't hurt them any longer. As if it was finally behind them, where it belonged.

As if, after everything, he trusted her again.

And so Holly melted into him, kissed him back, and for the first time in four and a half long years let herself believe things might be all right, after all.

"Well?" Demetrious Tsoukatos's gruff voice was more belligerent than usual over the phone line, which did not bode well. "Have you sorted out your marital issues yet? Or can I look forward to even more of this tabloid nonsense to give me indigestion?"

Theo stood out on the private balcony that ran along the side of the Chatsfield honeymoon suite, his eyes on the sun in the distance as it sank down into a riot of spring color arrayed along the horizon, and ordered himself to remain calm.

Or as calm as anyone could remain when talking to his father.

"You cannot possibly imagine my marriage is any of your business," he said when he was certain he could sound cool and unbothered, completely in control. "Let me assure you, if you are confused on that score, that it is not." He even laughed. "With all due respect, Father, yours is not the counsel I would ever voluntarily seek when it comes to matrimony."

"You are needed in Athens," his father barked at

him, the slight rasp in his voice the closest he ever got to a display of emotion. Theo considered it a direct hit. "You are meant to be running *my* company, not letting that girl parade you around Europe by your—"

"*That girl* is my wife whether you like it or not," Theo said icily, cutting the old man off before he could veer too far into the unforgivable. "And I am as interested in your thoughts on my marriage now as I was four and a half years ago, Father, when you boycotted my wedding and yet, somehow, it went ahead without you."

"Perhaps if you'd listened back then you wouldn't be in this crisis now!" his father retorted, sounding as guilt-free now as he had then. But, of course, Theo wasn't certain Demetrious knew what guilt was. "Splashed all over the papers and half the company— *my company*—at her greedy fingertips!"

"Why don't we continue this conversation when you have recalled that, once again, I did not ask for your opinion on my marriage," Theo said, very distinctly. "Or—and this is my preference—not at all. Make peace with this, Father, however you can. I don't care what you think about it."

"You must end this spectacle, Theo." His father's voice was dark, and wholly unmoved by anything Theo might have said, as always. The great Demetrious Tsoukatos cared about two things—himself and whatever made him more money. Theo knew better than to expect otherwise, and the truth was, the longer he spent with Holly, the less he cared what the old man did. "One way or the other."

"Goodbye, Father," Theo replied, and ended the call, tucking his mobile into the pocket of his trousers and letting the stunning Spanish sunset, pinks and deep blues cavorting magnificently over the old city before they succumbed to the coming dark, soothe the ragged things inside of him.

But he knew that there was only one thing that could truly do that, only one person who ever had, and he had stopped pretending otherwise.

They'd stood in that alley for a long time, kissing. Just kissing.

And it had changed everything.

He'd tasted her again and again, kissing her as if his life depended on it.

He rather thought it might, that was the trouble. Because it had been one thing to live out the past four years in a dark fury. Outraged at what she'd done to him and determined to *prove* he wasn't ruined by her deception, her betrayal. Determined to be unbroken, unchanged, by what had happened between them, he'd told himself almost daily—and yet he hadn't let her go, had he?

He wanted to let her go even less, now.

"That did not sound like a pleasant conversation," she said from behind him.

"Perhaps you've forgotten that my father is not a particularly pleasant man," Theo replied with a shrug. "Merely an effective one."

He turned to find her standing in the graceful doorway that led into the suite, and he thought she was far more beautiful than the sun's display over the distant hills and the gleaming sea. She was wearing his shirt like a robe, wrapped around her lovely form, with her hair a great and glorious mess around her shoulders, and his chest ached at the sight.

Maybe it would always ache when he saw her. Maybe that was the point.

They'd had a great deal of sex since that first time on the sofa, only a handful of days ago. It had been wild, intense. Deeply addictive. Perfect, every time, just as he remembered it from before.

But none of it had come close to what they'd shared this last time, when they'd come back here after their interlude in that alley in the Gothic Quarter, drunk on all that kissing. Intoxicated and filled with a new kind of light. A new kind of trust.

Sacred, he thought.

He had no intention of letting her go. None whatsoever. Not ever again.

"You must have things to do back in Athens," she continued after a moment, her hand on the door frame as if she needed to steady herself. Theo's gaze sharpened at that, and he felt everything inside him still. "You can't have planned for a vacation on the fly like this." She swallowed, hard, as if she was forcing down a reaction she didn't want him to see, shoving it out of his view before he could name it. "I don't want to keep you from your responsibilities, Theo."

He studied her then, all of his senses on high alert. The sunset played over her face, making her shine that little bit brighter, but he could see the shadows in her eyes. That stark vulnerability.

And he knew. He knew what she was going to do.

"Are you ready to return to Greece with me, Holly?" He leaned back against the rail behind him and kept his attention trained on her, and he did not ball his hands up into fists. He did not bellow his feelings into the twilight sky. He simply gazed at her and waited for this ax of hers to fall. "Is that what you're trying to say?"

"I think you should go to Greece right now if that's what you need to do," she told him, and he could see she meant that.

She wove her hands together in front of her, and he had the sudden, perfect recollection of her standing exactly like that four years ago as she'd spun her lies for him, devastating him in a few stark sentences. He hadn't paid much attention to her body language then, that she'd held her hands out like that when she never had before. But he'd had four years of angry mornings in his gym, remembering every single moment of that last night and every tiny thing she'd done as she'd ripped out his heart and stomped on it.

Tonight, he knew what it was.

Fear. Again.

"You are too kind," he murmured.

Holly's troubled blue gaze met his, then danced away again.

"I think these days together have been enormously instructive," she said, and her voice changed as she spoke. She stood taller, held herself more elegantly. He supposed this was the Holly Tsoukatos who dominated all the charities she was involved with. Remote. Inaccessible. Unemotional—but he could see her eyes.

He could see *her*, no matter what she said. "I think we've learned that we do, in fact, have something to build on, after all. Maybe we should take a month or so to reflect on everything that's happened, and then craft a reasonable way to move forward."

"Or," he said softly, "you can just come home with me. And then stay there, the way you should have done from the start."

"Oh!" Her face flushed red and her eyes went wide, as if he'd suggested something shocking. "I don't think—"

"Holly." He said her name, just her name, and her voice cut off as if he'd barked out a harsh command. He met her gaze and held it. Tried to will her not to do this thing he knew very well she was planning to do. He could *see* it, written there over her face as if she'd inscribed the words in blood, right there on the perfect slopes of her cheeks. "Come home, *agapi mou*. It's time."

CHAPTER TEN

THEO DIDN'T KNOW what he expected, only what he wished with every last shred of himself, yet Holly only stared back at him for a long, shuddering sort of moment, something much too much like misery making her blue eyes look dark.

"No," she said, her voice thick. "I can't, Theo. I can't go to Greece."

She didn't wait for him to form a response to that, or even to see if he'd try. She spun around and disappeared back inside, throwing herself into the shadows of the suite's interior with a kind of desperate lurch that suggested she was unsteady on her own feet.

But it was the throwing herself away from him that he comprehended first, and it cut deep. She was escaping him as best she could, all over again, and it was hard not to bleed out a little bit at that. No matter that he'd seen this coming.

If anything, that made it worse. Because he should have known better than to kiss her like that, to make love to her like that. Pain and cruelty and uncertainty drew her to him, made her run to him. Love made her run away. These days together in a city he would always think of as theirs made that clear to him.

He only wished he'd understood the truth of that years ago.

Theo stood where he was for a long moment, then another. When he had that bright red thing within him under control again, shoved back down deep and bound up tight, he followed Holly into the bedroom, not at all surprised to find her pulling her clothes back on in a frenzied sort of hurry.

As if, were she to delay even a second, she'd be lost.

He'd peeled off that blouse she was shrugging back on slowly, so slowly. He'd tasted every last millimeter of the skin he'd bared as he went. Her collarbone, her elegant neck. That sweet, soft place where her arm met her shoulder and veered off toward her breast. Only when she'd moaned beneath him had he moved to strip off the bra she'd worn, baring those dark-tipped breasts to his view—to his mouth—at last.

He should have kept her naked, the animal in him growled. Maybe then he'd have kept her close.

"Where are you going?" Theo asked, his voice as light as he could make it, but he knew. He already knew. He could see the panic and the darkness fighting it out in the storm inside her gaze, in the careful way she held her mouth, as if she worried a sob might escape if she wasn't careful.

"You need to get back to your business and I'm needed in Dallas."

"By whom?"

Her eyes had that sheen in them, that hectic sparkle, that gave him all the answers he needed. But he didn't relent. He couldn't.

"I have responsibilities," she told him, but she dropped her gaze as she said it, looking around the bedroom as if the tossed-back sheets and well-used mattress might offer her a clue.

He almost felt sorry for her, Theo thought. He was almost sympathetic. But he was standing there in nothing but a pair of boxer briefs and his body was still pleasantly worn-out from all the ways he'd explored her, cherished her, taken her. *Worshipped her.* He'd kissed away the tears that had leaked from behind her closed eyes when she'd shattered in his arms. When she'd moaned out her pleasure and he'd heard nothing but love in the sound. But he doubted she'd let him do it now.

"Do you?" He watched her move around the room, every part of her vibrating with a terrible tension, as if she was holding back a personal, internal earthquake by sheer force of will alone. Perhaps she was. If he wasn't so angry with her, with what she was about to do *again*, he thought he might ache for her. "And what responsibilities are those, exactly?"

She stopped moving then, and threw her hands out. "Stop!" she hissed at him, as if he couldn't see the way her hands shook, undercutting anything she might say. "Just let me go."

"But you see, that is the trouble," Theo replied, making his voice lazy, forcing his body to lean against the doorjamb as if he felt anything like at his ease.

"I've already let you go once. I don't particularly want to do it again."

"This was a mistake," she muttered. "This was all a god-awful mistake."

"Which part, Holly?" He watched her shove her hands in her hair, saw the conflicted expression that moved over her face, sad and lost and wounded, and he wondered how he'd missed it the first time around. Had he truly been so narcissistic four years ago? Had he seen nothing at all but his own pain, his own ego? But he knew he had. He'd watched her do exactly this and *he'd believed her*. On some level, Theo thought then, that was the greatest betrayal of all. If he'd known her at all, he should have known better. "The part where you love me so much it terrifies you? Or the part where you don't know how to love at all unless it hurts?"

She breathed in something ragged that sounded a good deal like a sob, but there was something else in her stormy gaze. Something like steel. Resignation and regret.

"Maybe love simply hurts because that's what it does," she flared at him. "Maybe everything between us is too painful for a reason. I lied to you. You slept around. None of that could ever have happened if we were anything remotely resembling good for each other!"

"Holly." He straightened from the doorjamb and waited for her to look at him again. He watched the way she trembled and he couldn't think of anything he wanted more than to go to her, to gather her close, to soothe away this latest storm of hers—but he didn't. "You believe that love *should* hurt. That the only way you can possibly know if it's love in the first place is if it's crippling. If you worry it might break you. So if the hurt doesn't exist on its own, you invent it."

Her mouth fell open and she stopped trembling with a suddenness, an abruptness, that was almost like a gunshot through the quiet room around them.

"Is that a roundabout way of telling me I'm crazy?" she asked, but her voice had gone cold. It was pure ice, all the way through, and Theo understood it. He understood her for the first time, he thought, her and him and everything that had happened between them then and now—and that was why he couldn't let this go the way so much of him longed to do.

"Not at all," he said. "We are all what we were raised to be, are we not? Though we claim that will never happen to us, that we'll fight it with our dying breaths, that we take only what we like from our parents and no more. Yet I am my father's son, for better or worse. Just as you are your father's daughter."

She sucked in another too-harsh breath, and it was loud. So loud he thought it must have hurt her. It hurt him, too.

"Be careful, Theo," she warned him then. "My father was a good man. A good man and a true one to the very end. He's not ammunition you can use to make a point." Her eyes flashed, darkening, and her pretty mouth trembled. "Any good thing there might be in me, he taught me."

"He taught you how to mourn," Theo contradicted

her with gentle deliberateness that was no less accurate for its softness, and she stiffened. "He taught you how to make a whole life into a monument to a selfish woman who wanted neither one of you."

"He *loved* her!" Holly cried.

"Just as my mother loved my father, and to what end?" His own voice was merciless then, Theo knew, but he couldn't stop. "Love is a living thing, Holly. Don't you see that? It's not set in stone. It's not a test of endurance designed only to break you. You can love me without all this darkness. Without the pain and the loss and the grief. You can simply love me, I promise."

She let out a sound far too painful to be a laugh, and it tore at him. It wrecked him as surely as a lie had four years ago. "How would you know? What evidence is there to support that? Not one thing in our history suggests we can do anything but fall apart."

"Those six months in Santorini were the best of my life," he told her, holding her gaze, letting her see the very heart of him. "There was no darkness. There was no fear. There were no others between us, real or imaginary. And we were *happy*." He let that sink in for a breath. "That was why you ran, wasn't it? It's not losing yourself you fear. It's finding yourself whole. Whole and happy and loved. The way your father never could."

And he couldn't say he was particularly surprised when she blanched at that, jerking back as if he'd hit her and going terribly, alarmingly pale besides.

No more, everything inside of him shouted, wild

and snarling at the restraint he was showing. *You should be the one who protects her, not the one who attacks her!*

"Holly…"

"Enough!" she threw at him, though her voice was but a strangled whisper, and she hardly sounded like herself. She sounded as wrecked as he felt. As if they'd crushed each other to pieces all over again. Shards of glass, ground into dust. "You've said enough, Theo. More than enough. I can't hear any more of this."

And this time, she didn't sneak out while he slept. She didn't run away while he wasn't looking, leaving him to pick up what pieces remained and then stitch himself back together with whatever fury and heartbreak and grief she'd left behind her.

Not this time.

This time, Holly walked swiftly away from him and she didn't look back. She didn't glance over her shoulder, and she was still so alarmingly pale it was as if she'd become her own ghost.

And Theo let her go.

Holly was halfway across the gleaming, fresh-scented lobby of The Harrington before she realized that someone was calling her name—and that it wasn't Theo, the only person she both wanted to hear and wanted to avoid, all at the same time.

More than that, she wanted to die. More accurately, she thought she'd *already* died and wanted nothing more than to hide herself away in some corner somewhere and collapse… Maybe then, she'd stop *feeling* all of this. Maybe then, she'd make sense of the mad tilt and crash that was still happening inside of her.

But instead of heading up to her room to find that corner, she stopped, pasting what she hoped was a smile on her face and aiming it at the woman who marched toward her, wearing the trim suit and gold-edged nametag of a Harrington employee.

"Mrs. Tsoukatos," the woman said in an efficient British accent. "I am so sorry. I'm the day manager here and I wanted to make certain I apologized to you personally for the grievous and unacceptable breach of your privacy. I spent the morning on the telephone with our CEO, Isabelle Harrington, who was deeply concerned and appalled and asked me to extend an apology both on behalf of The Harrington in general and from her in—"

"Forgive me," Holly interrupted before her head exploded, all over the shiny floor and the tasteful flower arrangements that tossed scent and color around like confetti and made her feel somehow more exposed because of it, "but I have no idea what you're taking about."

The woman stood straighter, her polite expression intact, if more careful. She cleared her throat and Holly didn't bolt, because thinking about something—anything—besides Theo and her marriage and the stunning mess she'd made of her life seemed like a gift. A reprieve.

"I'm afraid that the recent attention you've received in the papers was a direct result of the inappropriate actions of one of our Harrington employees," the woman said, and on some level, Holly admired the way she got right to the point. "Obviously we've removed this gentleman from his position and are considering what further disciplinary actions might be appropriate." She paused and coughed delicately. "If it helps at all, he thought he was helping the hotel, in direct response to similar actions from an employee at The Chatsfield. He didn't realize his actions could be interpreted as an unacceptable attack on one of our hotel guests. I don't expect this to make a difference to you, Mrs. Tsoukatos, nor should it when you've been victimized by his poor decision-making, but his heart truly was in the right place."

"What does that mean? What does a heart have to do with it? With anything?" Holly asked without realizing she meant to speak. She saw the other woman's smooth brow crease and, worse, saw her own reflection in one of the great mirrors rimmed in deep, old gold that lined the far wall.

She looked like a lunatic. That was a fact. She looked unkempt and wild—very much as if she'd spent all day rolling around in bed with a man and had then raced off across the city to get away from him without so much as taking a comb to her hair.

Which, of course, she had.

If she was honest, she looked the way she'd always looked, way back when. *Like a regular person*, a small voice whispered then. No hours spent bored to tears in salons achieving the kind of high gloss that screamed *high-class* to the sorts of people who

cataloged such things. No ruthless armor of the right
clothes, the right shoes, even the right facial expres-
sions, to blend in with the kind of women who lived
the life Holly did following her departure from Santorini. The empty and terribly, terribly shiny life she'd
made for herself in the years since she'd left Theo.

It's not losing yourself you fear, he'd said—but she
couldn't let herself think about that. She couldn't let
his words take root. She was too afraid that once they
did, once they leveled her completely, there would be
nothing left.

"Excuse me," Holly said then, before the other
woman could try to cover the awkwardness that hung
between them with more apologies. "I appreciate your
apology, I do. But I'm afraid I must check out. Immediately."

"While The Harrington fully understands your
position, Mrs. Tsoukatos, and regrets it, I want to
assure you that steps have been taken and will continue to be taken to make certain that this kind of…"

Holly shook her head, raising a hand to her temple,
and the woman cut herself off.

"Please," Holly whispered, and for once she didn't
care what she sounded like. Or even if anyone overheard her. "Have a car out front in ten minutes."

"Of course," the woman said.

And finally Holly spun away, making for the elevator bank and hoping against hope that she could slip
inside before the fog taking over her sight spilled out
into tears. *You mean* more *tears*, she reminded herself sharply, but she didn't want to think about that,

either. The way Theo had cradled her in his arms, still moving so slow and deep inside of her, holding her close while she shattered. While she broke. While she lost herself and everything she'd thought she knew…

Holly jabbed the button repeatedly, aware that she was in a panic, that everyone else in the lobby could no doubt *see* that she was losing it—but then, as she felt the hint of heat at the corners of her eyes, a kind of desperate chill stole over her, and just like that, she didn't care.

She didn't care about anything, she thought firmly—*fiercely*—as the elevator doors finally opened and she catapulted herself inside, squeezing her eyes shut and breathing hard as she rode up toward her suite. She didn't care what anyone thought of her, she told herself as she burst into her room and packed her things in a wild, frenetic whirl, as if she thought demons might descend upon her and carry her off if she wasn't out of the hotel in mere moments. She didn't care what she thought of *herself*, she assured herself as she lugged her own bags back down to the lobby and into the waiting car, because that hardly mattered any longer when she was fairly certain she'd left the last bit of who she was in Theo's bed. In his arms.

She wrapped herself in the pashmina she always carried in her travel bag, though it was anything but cold on such a warm summer's evening. Then she curled up in the backseat of the car, and she directed the driver to take her to the airport as quickly as he could, and then, only then, did she cry.

She cried and she cried.

And Holly didn't care about that—about indulging in an emotional breakdown in a semipublic place, no matter that the car's windows were tinted—either. Because the truth was, she didn't care about anything but putting as much distance between her and Theo as possible.

She couldn't care about anything else, because she couldn't *think* of anything else.

It's not losing yourself you fear, he'd said, damn him, and she could hear him as plainly as if he was sitting right there with her in the car, next to her in the leather bucket seats. She could *see* him as if he was still delivering those words to her like a prison sentence from up on high, looking at her with challenge and pity and some other dark thing in his gaze she was afraid to identify. *It's finding yourself whole. Whole and happy and loved.*

She wrapped her arms around herself, and let the past wash over her. Her sad, lonely childhood, spent alone on their remote spit of ornery Texas land, just Holly and her mournful father and the ghost of the woman who had wanted neither one of them at all.

Her earliest memories were of the relentless, endless chores and her own guilt that her father had her to deal with in addition to the land that gave him so little. Guilt and shame that her mother hadn't wanted her enough to take her or fight for her or even keep in touch with her once she'd gone. And guilt that no matter how hard she'd worked, no matter how dedicated she'd been to him, her father had never loved her as much as he'd loved the land itself and the woman who'd left him there to rot on it.

In the car, hurtling toward the airport, Holly sucked in a sharp breath, one hand moving to massage that hollow place that had opened up in her chest.

Oh, her father had loved her. Holly knew that he had, as much as he'd been able. As much as he'd had left in him.

But Theo had been right. Her father's love had been a furious thing, wounded and scarred. It had been love laid prostrate to someone who would never want him back, much less love him in return. It was a life lived for the one who left, not the ones who stayed behind.

And it had never occurred to Holly to question that. It had never crossed her mind to think about how unhealthy that kind of life was. She'd shut down any thoughts of her upbringing a long time ago. She'd refused to think of her father as anything but the good man she knew he was. Because that part was true. He was a good man, a decent man. He had a deep sort of faith and he'd treated others fairly, and he'd taught Holly to do the same.

But he was a man first, a human being, and those were complicated creatures, never all one thing or another. Gabe Holt had been harsh and silent. Stubborn like the damned land that had broken him down year in and year out. And he had never let go, not of anything—the ranch, his wife, his determination—no matter how much it hurt him. No matter what damage it did. No matter if it was hard to tell, after a decade or two, if it was love or hate that drove him.

"Stop," Holly whispered, and she didn't know who she was talking to any longer.

The ghosts in her past? The unhealthy creature who squatted in her mind and insisted she had to be as unhappy as the people who'd raised her? That their brand of pain was familiar and that made it better, somehow? Or at least right?

That if she wasn't racked with pain, she wasn't alive?

Outside the windows, the day was bright. Warm. And yet she was still so cold.

And Holly knew then that all of this was her fault. That no matter what Theo might have done, she'd done it first.

Because Theo had loved her, deeply and passionately, from the moment they'd met. He'd fought his family. Ignored his critics. He'd been a famous playboy before her and yet when he'd found her, he'd been utterly faithful until she'd convinced him she wasn't. It had been her lie, her determination to escape their marriage because she was afraid of losing herself, that had caused all of this.

She had never understood, until now, that what she was afraid of losing was the pain.

The pain she'd been raised with. The deep hurt that infused every last moment of her childhood. The agony had hung like smoke in the dark rooms of her childhood home, sneaking into her clothes, her skin. It had pressed into her and weighed her down like the famous Texas heat, until she'd had no idea that it *wasn't* a part of her. Until she'd believed that, without it, she was unrecognizable.

Because without it, Holly didn't know who she was. The society maven, capable of extraordinary elegance even when she used it as armor? Or the unsophisticated, untutored naïf who had careened around Europe in her own dizzy bubble, which she hadn't understood until now was its own kind of costume?

She didn't know who she was, but for the first time in as long as she could remember, Holly had a very clear idea of who she wanted to be instead.

And that was why she didn't shake at all when she sat up straight and wiped her eyes. When she tucked her pashmina back in her bag and smoothed down the blouse she remembered Theo removing with such bone-melting patience.

That was why her voice was strong and smooth when she asked the driver to turn them around and take her back into the city, after all.

To The Chatsfield, Barcelona.

To Theo, if he'd have her.

CHAPTER ELEVEN

HOLLY HAD NO particular plan.

She arrived at the hotel, had the porters deal with her luggage, and then she was standing there once more, surrounded by gleaming marble on all sides, sparkling chandeliers above, everything so perfectly luxurious it made her try to breathe more quietly, the better to blend.

You're stalling, she acknowledged.

Her rings caught the dancing light from above her, and Holly stared at them the way she had when Theo had first put them there, high on a cliff with only the gorgeous Greek sea below. She remembered the way they'd caught her eye, so bright and happy, just like the fizzy way she'd felt inside every time she'd looked at Theo.

She remembered how powerful she'd found the wearing of them, because they were more than simply pretty stones set against graceful bands. They were more than jewelry. They were promises forged into precious metal.

They were vows that were never meant to come off.

And she might have broken her promises in a hundred ways since she'd made them, but the rings were still right there. She'd never removed them, not in all these years. As if her subconscious had been trying to tell her the truth this whole time.

It was time to make good on that truth. Past time.

She'd started toward the elevator when she heard a Greek curse, uttered in a rich, low voice she'd recognize anywhere. A voice that moved in her the way it always had and always would.

Like heat. Like home.

"Let me make something clear to you," Theo told a diffident hotel employee who stood before him as if awaiting—even anticipating—a hard kick. "I don't care about Spencer Chatsfield or his issues or the misbehavior of his employees. I want…"

Holly felt it when he saw her. It was harder than any kick. It lit her up, making her entire body shift into bright red.

Theo waved the Chatsfield man away and moved toward Holly instead, his expression fierce at first and then, as he drew close, shuttered. She noticed his bags behind him on a golden hotel trolley and told herself that was nothing to be upset about. She'd left first.

"Where are you going?" she asked, and she had to swallow hard, her throat was so dry. "Back to Athens?"

He studied her for a moment in that way of his, as if he could see straight through her. As if he could see deep inside her bones. And for the first time, she welcomed it. Theo blinked.

"Yes," he said. "To Athens." He didn't reach out to her then, he simply shifted slightly, and Holly didn't know why she felt as if he'd touched her. As if he'd held her close, somehow, without even laying a finger on her. The corner of his mouth curved. "By way of Dallas."

Something uncurled inside of her, warm and fragile at once. It flooded her, making her feel weak and powerful all at once.

"I got the distinct impression that you were letting me go," she whispered. "And who could blame you?"

"I was," Theo agreed. "But I didn't say I wouldn't follow right behind you." He shook his head. "You were right, Holly, about so many things. I should have followed you then. I never should have let that last night stand as the only conversation we ever had about our marriage. I was filled with ego, with hurt pride…"

"How could you be anything else?" she said, all the things she'd waited all these years to say falling over one another as she tried to speak, to get them out at last. "You were the only person in all my life who loved me back, Theo. It terrified me. It still terrifies me. I don't know how to do anything but run as far away from it as I can, hurting both of us in the process. Again and again."

"But you keep coming back."

"Ineptly." She laughed, an uneven sound. "Half-assedly."

"Yet here you are," he pointed out, all that warmth

in his dark gaze making her feel wrapped in gold. Something like cherished, though she hardly dared think that word. "That must mean something."

He moved again, pulling her hands into his, and then, simply, everything was better. So much better, it was like moving from deep shadows into the bright noonday sun. It was cold become heat, that easily. Holly gazed down at his strong hands wrapped around hers, then up to his face again.

And it was as if they were thrown back in time, back to that breeze-touched cliff in all the soaring Santorini sunshine. His hands had held hers, just like this. She'd gazed up at him, just like this. And she'd made promises to him she'd never meant to break.

This time, she'd do it better, she vowed. This time, she'd stay strong.

"I love you," she told him then, and now, even as they mixed together in her head. "Though you have no reason to believe me."

"But I do," he murmured, taking one of her hands to his mouth and pressing a kiss there, like a boon. Like an act of faith, of love. "I do believe you. I believe you always have loved me, in your own way."

"I think you love me, too," she continued, her voice barely audible, though she knew he heard her when his dark eyes took on that bright golden gleam again, deeper and more powerful than before. "Though I can't think of a single reason why."

"I can think of a thousand," he assured her. "But I don't need reasons, Holly. I've always loved you. I always will. Reasons change behavior, perhaps, but they can't change a heart. And mine is yours. Still and always, yours."

"I want to love you the way I should," she told him fiercely. "I want to love you so much I never think of running again. I want to keep my promises to you, and never give you cause to break yours again." Her eyes stung then, but she forged on. "I want to go back in time and do it over, take it back…"

"We met and married too fast," Theo said, pulling her closer, so she propped herself against him with her hands on his chest. "We needed to grow up. Our problem is that we did this apart, that's all. Every couple must grow, Holly. That's the only way to survive." He shifted, running his hands along her sides, bringing them up to trace something like wings on her back, as if he thought she could fly if she wanted to and here, in his arms, she believed she could. *She believed.* "And we will survive. I have every confidence."

"How can you?" she asked, her voice small. "After everything that's happened?"

"Because this time it took you a mere hour to come back to me," he said, his fine mouth curving gently in one corner. "Next time, perhaps you won't leave at all. And that's what matters, Holly. Everything else, we have the rest of our days to work out as best we can. Fighting. Dancing. Rose petals and forced marches down memory lane…"

She slid her arms high and looped them around his neck, and though she could feel the cool kiss of tears against her cheeks, she smiled at him. She felt that smile all the way to her toes.

Because he looked like forever.

She thought that maybe, this time, that's what they were.

"That sounds tempting," she said now, tilting her head back and looking at him. Really *looking* at him. Her beautiful husband. Whom she would learn how to love without making it hurt like this, she promised herself then. Whom she would learn to love as he deserved, or die trying. "Or, of course, you could kiss me."

Theo's smile spread over his lean cheeks and lit up his eyes. It filled Holly's heart and spilled out everywhere else, making her shine. Making her feel as bright as he was, as if between them they burned brighter and hotter than the whole of the Spanish summer ahead.

She believed that, too.

"I could," he said softly. "I will. I promise you, Holly. I always will."

Theo made good on his word, tipping her back in his arms and kissing her senseless, right there in the middle of the luxurious marble lobby of The Chatsfield, Barcelona.

And neither one of them cared even the slightest bit if every last paparazzo alive was watching.

Five years later, Theo sprawled happily in the infinity pool of his private villa, set high on the Santorini cliffs, and permitted himself the simple joy of relaxing in the beautiful summer afternoon all around him.

They'd earned each and every scrap of happiness, he thought.

They'd spent the first year after their second honeymoon in Barcelona testing themselves. Could they trust each other? Could they grow together? Could they learn how to stay together, after all?

The simple answer was yes to all, but life was rarely simple. It took commitment. It took openness. Vulnerability and trust were at the core of intimacy, and intimacy took time. It built slowly.

And it was only sometimes about sex, which was too bad, as that still came as easy and as blistering as it always had.

Holly had been faced with the unenviable task of earning the trust of those who had never trusted her to begin with. Theo had had the pleasure of watching the brittle version of her fade, though she would never quite be the dizzy, naive girl he'd swept away so easily.

In the place of either of those, she was *his* Holly.

Warm and often sweet, though never a pushover. Filled with hope and laughter, as he'd always imagined she'd deserved to be. Smart enough to run the social side of a tycoon's life like its own ruthless corporation, wise enough to enlist the otherwise unapproachable Mrs. Papadopoulos to help her do it seamlessly and graciously.

She was a force to be reckoned with, his beautiful

wife—though, of course, he'd always thought so. Especially when he'd been the one doing the reckoning.

Holly had even won over his brother and his disapproving father, though the latter had taken almost the whole of these five years to come around. It helped that the old man had nothing to do any longer but sit around, count his olive groves and permit his pretty daughter-in-law to flatter him, Theo thought, but he smiled as he thought it, his eyes on the shifting sea down below him and the Greek horizon in the distance.

The mighty Demetrious Tsoukatos had retired, leaving Theo in his place, and it was perhaps only a surprise to Theo—and only in his more self-deprecating moments—that he was damned good at it. He'd made his hardworking brother, Brax, his right-hand man and he'd catapulted Tsoukatos Shipping straight into the glorious future they'd spent all these hard years earning.

All that rose must fall—before rising again, stronger than before.

This was who they were. This was what they did.

This was true happiness, Theo realized then. Pure happiness, emanating out from the deepest core of him, and it only got brighter when he heard her light steps on the stones behind him. He felt the silken water of the pool shift as she entered it, heard her splash slightly as she dunked her head as she always did when she slipped into the pool, and then, moments later, she was pressing herself against his back, wrapping her arms around him and resting her chin on his shoulder.

Theo waited until she let out a long, happy sigh, and knew her gaze, like his, was fixed on the horizon. On all that lay ahead of them.

On the future growing within her even now, that her visit to the doctor today had been meant to confirm.

"Well?" he asked.

"I have a confession to make," she said, her voice ripe with laughter and with love, with that teasing note he found he adored beyond reason. "I've finally taken it all the way."

He didn't know what she meant, not really, and so he simply held her hands as they gripped his chest, folding in together like their own Gordian knot. *Unbreakable*, he thought.

"Should I be concerned?"

"Only if you find it troubling to be tied to me forever in the time-honored fashion," she said, and the echo of his own harsh words, uttered so long ago across a restaurant table in Barcelona, came back to him. "I'm afraid that you really will be forced to play these games with me forever."

He leaned his head against hers and felt her breathe. He felt it move in him, too, like a wish. Like a prayer. Both already granted.

"Ah, *agapi mou*," he whispered. "You have given me everything. I want to give you the whole world."

"Silly man," she said, shifting to press her lips to

his skin, a moment before he pulled her into his arms and demonstrated his joy in the starkest and most emphatic terms possible. "You already did."

* * * * *

If you enjoyed this book,
look out for the next installment of
THE CHATSFIELD:
RUSSIAN'S RUTHLESS DEMAND
by Michelle Conder
Coming next month.

HARLEQUIN
Presents®

Whether you're in America, Australia, Europe or Dubai
our doors will always be open…

Welcome to
The Chatsfield
Synonymous with style, spectacle…and scandal!

The notorious Chatsfields have come together to make
The Chatsfield Hotel the most notorious, luxurious and desirous
location for the world's impossibly rich and exceptionally famous.

Passion and power, winning and succeeding, their legendary
exploits are a legacy that is impossible to resist.

Don't miss out on a single story!

Add them to your collection today!

www.Harlequin.com

HPCHATS2015

#3341 SHEIKH'S FORBIDDEN CONQUEST
The Howard Sisters
by Chantelle Shaw

Sultan Kadir Al Sulaimar's first duty must be to his country, but feisty helicopter pilot Lexi Howard's disregard for his command is somewhat...refreshing. Can the desert king resist making her his final—and most forbidden—conquest before his arranged marriage?

#3342 TEMPTED BY HER BILLIONAIRE BOSS
The Tenacious Tycoons
by Jennifer Hayward

Harrison Grant can't afford distractions with a high-stakes deal on the table, but his new assistant, Francesca Masseria, is a beautiful diversion. And what he's beginning to want from Francesca isn't part of her job description!

#3343 SEDUCED INTO THE GREEK'S WORLD
by Dani Collins

For Natalie Adams, an affair in Paris with billionaire Demitri Makricosta surpasses her *wildest* dreams! But the closer Natalie gets to emotions he's locked away, the more Demitri tries to distract her to ensure that seduction remains the *only* thing between them...

#3344 MARRIED FOR THE PRINCE'S CONVENIENCE
by Maya Blake

Jasmine Nichols is catapulted to the top of the prospective brides list when Prince Reyes discovers she's carrying his heir! Except Reyes's cold, tactical marriage is about to be jeopardized by their explosive chemistry and what he learns when he uncovers his new bride's secrets...

REQUEST YOUR
FREE BOOKS!

HARLEQUIN

Presents®

2 FREE NOVELS PLUS
2 FREE GIFTS!

YES! Please send me 2 FREE Harlequin Presents® novels and my 2 FREE gifts (gifts are worth about $10). After receiving them, if I don't wish to receive any more books, I can return the shipping statement marked "cancel." If I don't cancel, I will receive 6 brand-new novels every month and be billed just $4.30 per book in the U.S. or $5.24 per book in Canada. That's a saving of at least 13% off the cover price! It's quite a bargain! Shipping and handling is just 50¢ per book in the U.S. and 75¢ per book in Canada.* I understand that accepting the 2 free books and gifts places me under no obligation to buy anything. I can always return a shipment and cancel at any time. Even if I never buy another book, the two free books and gifts are mine to keep forever.

106/306 HDN GHRP

Name	(PLEASE PRINT)	
Address		Apt. #
City	State/Prov.	Zip/Postal Code

Signature (if under 18, a parent or guardian must sign)

Mail to the **Reader Service**:
IN U.S.A.: P.O. Box 1867, Buffalo, NY 14240-1867
IN CANADA: P.O. Box 609, Fort Erie, Ontario L2A 5X3

**Are you a current subscriber to Harlequin Presents® books
and want to receive the larger-print edition?
Call 1-800-873-8635 or visit www.ReaderService.com.**

* Terms and prices subject to change without notice. Prices do not include applicable taxes. Sales tax applicable in N.Y. Canadian residents will be charged applicable taxes. Offer not valid in Quebec. This offer is limited to one order per household. Not valid for current subscribers to Harlequin Presents books. All orders subject to credit approval. Credit or debit balances in a customer's account(s) may be offset by any other outstanding balance owed by or to the customer. Please allow 4 to 6 weeks for delivery. Offer available while quantities last.

Your Privacy—The Reader Service is committed to protecting your privacy. Our Privacy Policy is available online at www.ReaderService.com or upon request from the Reader Service.

We make a portion of our mailing list available to reputable third parties that offer products we believe may interest you. If you prefer that we not exchange your name with third parties, or if you wish to clarify or modify your communication preferences, please visit us at www.ReaderService.com/consumerschoice or write to us at Reader Service Preference Service, P.O. Box 9062, Buffalo, NY 14240-9062. Include your complete name and address.

HP15

"Look, I didn't plan to announce an engagement to you this evening."

"I'm not so sure you didn't, Max. It certainly seemed to trip off your tongue very easily—along with that very inventive plan to treat me to a Devilliers ring. Tell me, are we taking your private jet?"

He glared at her. "I didn't plan it. He just… *Dio*. You heard him."

Darcy's insides tightened as she recalled the sense of protectiveness that had arisen when Montgomery had baldly dissected Max's life. He'd remained impervious in the face of much worse provocation. *But this had been personal. About his family.*

Darcy stood up, feeling vulnerable. "I heard him, Max. The man clearly has strong feelings about the importance of family, but do you think he really cares if you're married or not?"

"He believes my perspective will be skewed unless I have

someone to worry about other than myself."

"So you fed me to him?"

He looked at her. "Yes."

"I'm just a means to an end—so you can get your hands on that fund."

Max looked at Darcy. Why did those words strike at him somewhere? Of *course* she was a means to an end. And that end was in sight.

"Yes, you *are*— I won't pretty it up and lie to you. But, Darcy, if you do this you won't walk away empty-handed. You can name your price."

She let out a short, curt laugh and it made Max wince inwardly. It sounded so unlike her.

"Believe me, no price could buy me as your wife, Max."

Max felt that like a blow to his gut, but he gritted out, "I'm not *buying* a wife, Darcy. I'm asking you to do this as part of your job. Admittedly it's a little above and beyond the call of duty…but you will be well compensated."

Darcy tossed her head. "Nothing could induce me to do this."

"Nothing…?" Max asked silkily as he moved a little closer, his vision suddenly overwhelmed with the tantalizing way Darcy filled out her dress.

She put out a hand. "Stop right there."

Max stopped, but his blood was still leaping. He'd yet to meet a woman he couldn't seduce. *Was he prepared to seduce Darcy into agreement?* His mind screamed caution, but his body screamed *yes!*

Don't miss
THE BRIDE FONSECA NEEDS by Abby Green,
available June 2015 wherever
Harlequin Presents® books and ebooks are sold.

www.Harlequin.com

HARLEQUIN

Presents®

Love the drama of duty vs desire and the shocking
arrival of a secret baby? Maya Blake's passionate
and powerful story is for you!

MARRIED FOR
THE PRINCE'S
CONVENIENCE

June 2015

Jasmine Nichols is catapulted to the top of the
prospective brides list when Prince Reyes discovers
she's carrying his heir! Except Reyes's cold,
tactical marriage is about to be jeopardized by
their explosive chemistry and uncovering
his new bride's secrets…